AN INSANE MIND

DAVID JOSEPH MYSTERIES
BOOK 4

TERENCE NEWNES

Published 2024 by Next Chapter

Cover art by Lordan June Pinote

Large Print Edition

PROLOGUE

THE MAN

HE HAD SAT and brooded for months now over the stupidity of people. He believed very strongly in what he had written and spoken about, but no one, least of all the authorities who should have shown concern, had taken him seriously. He knew that there was a very strong possibility that what he had proposed would take place; if not now, then definitely at some point in time. But *now* was the time for the authorities to understand the danger and put systems in place to eliminate the possibility of this happening, and it angered him that they just refused to understand. It seemed to him as though people preferred to be reactive instead of being proactive. The longer he brooded, the more it became apparent to him that the reason for the authorities not paying attention to the problem was because they did not think *him* believable. *'Well,' he thought to himself. 'I don't mind what they think of me. I don't care for their opinions, but I think that they should care about security, which is what I've been talking about!'*

From the time that he had aired his warnings and people had either just brushed them aside as being of no importance, or worse still had belittled the idea, the anger in him had grown and festered. Like a child with a small itchy wound, he had scratched and poked at it until it grew larger and larger and had started to fester. Now he no longer remembered that it had started as a small wound. In his mind, it was a large wound and had always been like that. He told himself again and again that it did not matter to him what they thought of him. *He* did not matter; it was the danger that mattered. Of course, he had been the one to think of that danger, which just showed how smart he was. The more he brooded about the indifference that they had shown to his brilliant concept, the more his mind burned to show them how right he was and how wrong they were.

One day he woke up with a voice in his head telling him that he now had to prove to them just how right he was. He was fully aware that the voice was his own, but he also knew that it spoke the truth. He had come up with something that seemed so simple and understandable, and yet was so brilliant because of its simplicity. *'Well,' he thought to himself. 'If they refuse to listen, then I will make them listen. After all, it is for the greater good for the greater number.'* He had a sudden fleeting thought that that saying did not make much sense in this context, but then he had always liked that saying! He always used a lot of adages and aphorisms in articles that he wrote for the newspapers.

He was determined now to cleanse and heal the festering wound permanently. He sat down and began to browse the net. The more he found on the net, the more he was convinced of what he had written and spoken about. It was as though the oracle had spoken. 'I *am* the oracle,' he thought grimly. He made notes as he browsed the web and he covered three pages with his neat handwriting. He wasn't going to commit any part of his plan to the computer. Everything would be handwritten and then destroyed. He hesitated at that point because another part of his mind was telling him that he should not be going down this road. But then the other part of his mind said, *'This is something that you have to do. It is the right thing to do because sometimes stupid people will only listen if they receive a severe jolt!'*

After a week of searching the net, he felt that he had all the information he needed to begin his plan.

He broke down his plan into three parts: 1. Identifying the materials that were needed. 2. Procuring the materials. 3. A safe hiding place for everything until the time came to use them. He added a note at the end which said that he would have to test out everything before finally proceeding. The sane part of his mind kept telling him that he should stop. But as the days went by, that voice grew dimmer and the spark in his mind that demanded vindication grew stronger and brighter.

He had already identified the materials he would need from his search of the net. It took him another week of research to figure out how he would procure the materials without arousing suspicion and without any purchase being traced back to him. It took him another two weeks after that before the safe hiding place was ready, and he was absolutely sure that no one would find it. There were two attack plans that he had prepared. The first one did not require any experimentation or tests to see if it would work, because it was something that was already tried and tested. All he would be doing was carrying out the same thing on a much larger scale. But for the actual physical implementation of the plan, he thought that he would maybe have to do a trial run. If the trial run was a success then it would also prove beyond doubt that what he had said about the lack of security was true.

To assuage the sane voice in his mind, he decided that he would wait for a month or two. If anything happened in that time to prove his case, then he would not go ahead with his plan and he would not carry out the trial run. But in the meantime, he would identify the target and carry out a surveillance to see what security was actually there and if he could circumvent that security. He was absolutely sure that the security would be minimal, but he would still check. After about two months, an incident did take place and he thought that now he would not need to carry out his plan. But when nothing was done to enhance security even after that incident, he silenced the voice that was telling him to stop and he concentrated all his energy on finalising his plan.

For the second attack plan, he would need to do a lot of fabrication work and he would need to carry out some tests and experiment with the stuff to be sure that it would work. But he was confident that he had the knowledge to do whatever was necessary. There were two parts to the second plan, unlike the first which was quite simple except for the security aspect. The second plan depended on a little bit of chemistry and also a simple delivery device. It was dangerous stuff that he would be handling and he would need to be extra careful, but he had done his research and he had purchased the safety equipment that he would need. He had already identified an outlying farm where he would carry out his tests on the animals there late at night. Beyond the farm was a wide-open area and so it would also be the ideal place for him to see if the delivery device worked properly.

It took him another three months to safely and anonymously procure all the necessary materials, except for one unplanned event. It required patience and planning but he had succeeded. He had found the names of small companies on the net that were into the manufacture of furniture and glass. He had selected the ones that were located in far off districts and some in the neighbouring state as well. He had gone to each place and had visited each company on the pretext of buying some of their products. He would then say that he was in the process of starting his own company to make similar products and he would make sure to meet the owner. He would strike up a conversation with the owner about the methods used for production. He would invite the owner out for an evening of drinks or if the owner did not drink, then he would suggest a dinner. He would later ask to buy a small quantity of the powder so that he could experiment with it before he started his actual production.

He would casually offer twice or thrice what the powder was worth and he would act as though he was indebted to the owner for being so generous as to let him have a small quantity of the powder. In most of the cases, it worked and he got what he was after. In some cases, the owner would refuse, saying that the substance was dangerous and could not be resold. In such cases, he would not push but would readily agree with the owner and say, 'Better safe than sorry.' He had printed different business cards, each with a false name and address and he was absolutely sure that no one would ever be able to trace him even if the owners became suspicious and filed a complaint. He also resorted to small subtle disguises for all the visits. When meeting one owner he would sport a neat moustache and well-trimmed beard; for another meeting he would have only a moustache with long sideburns and he would wear glasses. He also made use of cheek pads to alter his features and once he went as a Sikh with a full growth of facial hair and wearing a turban. He had no doubt that the police would never be able to identify him as the man who bought the powder, at least, not based on any description that the factory owners could give.

The one unplanned incident that happened was when he visited a factory located in a rural place in the neighbouring state. The owner was a heavy drinker and the Man took him to a local bar and plied him with alcohol. The owner then took him to the factory and showed him where he kept the powder. "I have plenty," he told the Man. "You're a nice guy and so I'll give you two kilograms of the stuff. I hope you succeed in your venture." The Man thanked him and took the two kilos, but he also noted that there was no security and it would be easy to enter the factory through a window at night. He left the place but returned after three days in a rented car. He broke into the factory at night and stole more than thirty kilograms of the powder. The owner never reported the theft because he knew that he would face all sorts of trouble for not properly safeguarding such a dangerous substance.

After procuring the powder, it took another three months before he had perfected the chemistry and the fabrication work on the delivery device for the second attack. He did all purchases and fabrication works in far away districts. Nothing was purchased or done locally. He did his surveillance and trial run for the first attack and he was satisfied with the result. He tried out the efficacy of the delivered product for the second attack at the distant lonely farmhouse and then he tried out the delivery device in a desolate area beyond the farmhouse that stretched for miles with no nearby habitation. He chose a night when the air was still and humid to try out the device. Now he was ready and he was exultant. *'Soon,' he thought. 'Very soon now they will know just how wrong they were and how right I was! They will finally recognise my genius, but most of all they will finally be forced to recognise the danger and they will have to take action. That will justify my actions because the ends will justify the means.'* He realised suddenly that that was also one of his favourite sayings. He went to the calendar and picked a date for the first attack!

A DAY OF INSANITY

MAY 14, FRIDAY - 10:55 A.M.

"DADDY," shouted out little Suganya. "The water is coming!" She was a cute nine-year-old girl who loved her parents but was also a little bit mischievous. Her parents had forbidden her to drink water from the taps at school and on the roadsides. They had drilled it into her that for health reasons she should only drink filtered water. But most of her friends drank from the taps and they insisted that the water was tastier than filtered water. Little Suganya, however, obeyed her parents and did not drink water from the taps. But now as she looked at the cool water gushing from the pipe into the sump tank, she was tempted; and so cupping a little water in her palms she drank it and then drank again. But she would turn out to be one of the lucky ones! In hundreds of houses, that day at 11 a.m., people thanked God and the water department for the water, since it had been fifteen days since the last supply.

Sarala, a housewife in Ram Nagar, waited for five minutes for the water to fill a little in the sump and then switched on the motor to pump the water to the overhead Sintex tank that was placed on the terrace of their building. From there the water would come down to the house taps through a network of pipes. She waited for another five minutes and then opened the tap to fill the stainless steel tub in the kitchen. She waited impatiently for enough water to gather in the tub as she had to start her cooking for the day. She had been thinking of buying some tanker water as there was absolutely no potable water in the house since the day before. They were drinking and cooking with bottled water that they had to buy from the local grocer. She thanked all the Gods that at last the water had come because buying tanker water would have eaten into her budget, and at present they just could not afford it. She started the cooking, but before that, she made coffee for herself and her husband. She had two children, both boys, and because of the coffee, their lives were spared.

Aleem was about to leave for the mosque when the water came. He had been waiting for it and hoping that it would not be too delayed. He shouted out to his wife, “They have released the water! Wait for half an hour and then put on the motor. I am going to the mosque in a little while.” He lived with his wife, two children, and his elderly mother in a small house in Anbu Nagar. He did not know it at the time, but he would come back from the mosque to an empty house.

In Anbu Nagar, most of the lower-income group, like daily wage labourers and household maids, lived in what was called line houses or row houses. This was basically a long rectangular building partitioned along its length to make small homes that consisted of just two rooms each, one behind the other, and a tiny toilet. One row house would typically be divided into around five or six small homes which would be given on rent cheaply to people of the lower-income group, and Anbu Nagar had about ten such row houses. Each row house had one common potable water connection and the residents would line up and take their turn to fill the drums and buckets in their small homes with potable water.

In one such row house, there was a fight going on between two residents, Kamala and Shobha. Kamala told Shobha, “You have come here just two months ago and already you are causing problems for everyone! You know that we have a rotation system in place to draw the water from the tap when it comes. That way everyone has an equal chance of getting a little extra water whenever the corporation extends the time before shutting off the supply. But last time you bullied poor Jayanthi and put your pots and buckets before hers even though it was her turn to be first in the queue!" Shobha was a big-made arrogant woman and her husband was a small-made mild-mannered man, so she was used to getting her way in everything.

Now she shouted at Kamala, "You need to mind your own business! That is something between Jayanthi and myself, so what has it to do with you? Just shut your mouth and go about your business! Today it is my turn to be first in the queue and I'd like to see if you can stop me!" Kamala was a decent honest woman of around 55 years of age who always acted as a mediator in disputes between the families who occupied the row house. Now she told Shobha, "Are you daring to threaten me? If you continue in this way then I promise you that I will see to it that you are evicted from this place. Go and cause trouble somewhere else!" Jayanthi was a quiet, withdrawn person who hated fights and now she intervened and told Kamala, "Let it be mother, let her take the water first. This is not worth fighting over and you know that you have to think of your blood pressure."So when the water came, Shobha triumphantly started to fill her containers first; and just to rub it into the others, she took a big mug full of water and drank it right there in front of everyone. She was unaware of it at the time, but her arrogance would help to save the others!

Sanjana also lived in Anbu Nagar and she and her husband owned the house they lived in. It was a small house that they had built together with the help of some of her husband's friends, but she was very proud to live in her own house. Her husband Babu was a house painter and she brought in some extra money by doing tailoring at home. They had three small children, a boy and two girls; Raju, at seven years of age, was the eldest and was an active little boy, Divya was five and Deepa was just three years old. When the water came that morning, Sanjana was at her sewing machine completing some urgent work for a neighbour. Her son Raju shouted from the door, "Mother, the good water has come!" Sanjana immediately jumped up and ran outside. The tailoring would have to wait because the water was more important.

They did not have an underground sump and their connection was just outside the back door. The pipe had a tube connected to it that went into a large drum so that no water would be wasted if the water came earlier than expected. She had all the buckets and pots also lined up before the pipe and they had another large drum inside the small kitchen. She took the tube and filled the buckets and pots and then placed the tube back into the drum. Then she began carrying the buckets and pots one by one into the house and covering each one as she lined them up against the wall.

All three children were at the back and Divya started scooping water from a bucket with her small hands and drinking it. Raju was keeping a watchful eye on little Deepa and he told Divya, “Mother has told us not to drink the water until she boils it. I am going to tell her what you did!” She thumbed her nose at him and ran into the house. When his mother came out again he told her, “Divya drank the water from the bucket!” Sanjana shook her head in frustration and said, “Let me finish this work and I will deal with her. You be a good boy and don’t drink the water until I boil it.” By the time she had finished filling the water she had forgotten about the incident because she had to immediately go back to her sewing.

Sandra Smith lived in Vivek Nagar with her husband and two teenage daughters. Her husband was at work that day, and being the summer holidays, the children were at home and driving her crazy as usual. She had just agreed that they could go and visit their friend in the nearby area of Cheran Nagar when the water came. Her daughter Susan asked her, “Shall we wait and help you Mama?” Sandra said with a wry smile, "You're going to help me to put on the motor switch? I'm going to watch the TV for an hour and then I'll start on the lunch. You two go and visit your friend and I'll have lunch ready by the time you get back." They were one of the lucky families that day.

11:30 A.M

SUGANYA WAS a good child who always obeyed her parents, and this little act of disobedience in drinking the water from the pipe troubled her conscience. After about twenty minutes, she began to feel some discomfort in her stomach, and she thought that God must be punishing her for disobeying her parents. It was her father's day off from work, so both her parents were at home. Her father was watching television while her mother had started preparing lunch. Suganya went to her father and told him, "Daddy, I have been a bad girl!" Her father, Mukesh, smiled at his only child, whom he doted on, and said, "You can never be a bad girl, my sweet one!" But Suganya did not smile in return and said, "When the water came, I drank some water from the pipe and now my stomach is paining!"

She broke down and began crying, and her father shouted out to his wife, "Rohini, come here!" His wife came running from the kitchen, and Mukesh told her what Suganya had said. She went and hugged her daughter and told her, "Don't worry, little one, we all do bad things at times. But now that you have told us, all is forgiven and you can be sure that God forgives you too." But Mukesh said, "Rohini, I am not worried about that! She says that her stomach is paining." Suganya looked at her mother and said, "I think that God is punishing me for being disobedient!"

Rohini gave her husband a worried look and said, "Do you think the water is contaminated?" Mukesh shook his head and said, "I don't know, but let's not take any chances. Give her a concentrated salt water solution to drink to make her vomit, and then I will take her to the doctor." His wife ran to make the solution, and he shouted out to her, "And don't use that water until we find out if it is okay!" By 11.30 a.m. they rushed little Suganya to the nearby clinic, where they again gave her a stomach lavage and started a rehydration drip. Little Suganya's disobedience saved the lives of her family that day, and she also survived since they had treated her immediately.

11:45 A.M

SARALA and her husband drank their coffee leisurely. Sarala told her sons, "The water will have to fill in the overhead tank before I can fill the tub in the kitchen fully and then fill the water filter. You boys can drink the remaining bottled water today." Her husband said, "I will have to get ready in another hour or so as you know I have afternoon duty today." Sarala started to get up and said, "I will get the lunch ready." But her husband, Rakesh, said, "Relax! Sit down and enjoy your coffee. Even if the lunch is not ready it's no big deal as I can eat in the factory canteen." By 11.30 a.m. Sarala was preparing lunch when she suddenly felt nauseous. She turned off the gas and ran to the bathroom.

After vomiting copiously, she came to the living room to find her husband curled up on a couch holding his stomach. She told him, “I just vomited so much! What is wrong, Rakesh?” He looked at her and said, “My stomach is hurting so much I just cannot bear it!” She looked at him and saw him clench his teeth against the pain. “We will go right now to the hospital,” she told him. But just as she said that, she felt another wave of nausea hit her. She ran to the bathroom, but she did not make it and vomited on the dining room floor. She collapsed in a chair, and her husband came and pulled her up. “You lie down on the bed,” he told her. “I will go for the doctor.” Helping each other, they made it to the bedroom and collapsed on the bed. Then Rakesh vomited, and Sarala began retching. Their sons looked into the room with fear written large on their small faces, and their father told them, “Go outside and ask someone for help. Tell them we are very sick and we need a doctor. Go now!” The young boys ran outside the house and looked around for someone they could ask for help, and then they heard the screaming start in the neighbouring houses.

Aleem left for the mosque at 11.00 a.m. By 11.15 a.m. his wife switched on the motor and then started cooking lunch. Her elderly mother-in-law called out to her, “Daughter, this heat is killing me. Please give me a big glass of fresh water to drink.” Aleem’s wife, Ameena, thought it was a good idea.

She filled a jug with the fresh water and went to the dining room. She gave a big glass of water to her mother-in-law, her two young sons drank a glass each, and so did she. By 11.45 a.m. they were crying with stomach pain and cramps and nausea. Ameena made it to the phone and called a taxi driver who was her husband's friend. He was nearby and came to the house in his taxi within five minutes, and by 11.55 a.m. the entire family was admitted to the nearby clinic, where they were given stomach lavages and intravenous drips. Ameena and the boys survived, although they suffered complications for a long time, but her mother-in-law died within two hours.

The doctor who treated them at the clinic was the same doctor who had just treated little Suganya, and he told his nurse, "That little girl was from Ram Nagar, you said?" The nurse agreed, and the doctor remarked, "But this family is from Anbu Nagar, and they seem to have similar symptoms." He thought for a moment and then told her, "If I get even one more such case, we will call the local police station and inform them, but let's not create unnecessary panic right now. We will wait and see if any more similar cases come in."

Shobha from Anbu Nagar had defiantly drunk a full mug of water, and by 11.30 a.m. she had fallen in front of her rooms and was vomiting copiously. The residents were still filling the water, and Kamala ran over to her and asked, "What is wrong, Shobha, did you eat something bad? What are you feeling now, any pain, headache, tell me!" Shobha groaned and mumbled, "I did not eat anything...only curd rice...my stomach...pain...I'm dying..." Kamala stared at her for a long moment and then shouted out to the others, "No one is to drink that water! Hear me now! Do not let anyone drink that water." Jayanthi asked her, "Why, Kamala mother, what is wrong?" Kamala told her, "Shobha drank a full mug of that water in front of us and now she is vomiting and having stomach pains, so there must be something in that water." She told one of the men standing in the queue, "Please go and bring a rickshaw, and we will take her to the doctor." But Shobha died in the auto rickshaw before she reached the hospital. The rest of the people in that row house lived because of Kamala's quick thinking.

Around 11.30 a.m. little Divya started vomiting and crying that her stomach was hurting. Sanjana had just started her sewing again, and she put down her work and rushed to her daughter. She felt her forehead, but Divya did not seem to have a temperature, so she gave her some boiled water that was cooled and kept in an earthen jar for drinking. Divya seemed to feel a little better, so Sanjana made her lie down and went back to her sewing machine.

But within ten minutes, Divya started to vomit again, and then she fainted. Sanjana was desperate because her husband was away on a painting contract, and he would not be back until late that evening. She told Raju, "Hold on tight to Deepa, we are going to the clinic." She carried little Divya, and with Raju holding on tight to Deepa's hand, they started walking to the local clinic. They reached the clinic by 11.50 a.m., and the doctor immediately started a drip for the child, but Divya died at 12.05 p.m. This was the same doctor who had treated Suganya and Aleem's family, and he went and phoned the police to report what was happening. "I don't know if this is widespread or what exactly it is," he told the police. "But I treated a little girl around 11.30 and then a family came in with the same symptoms, and now another little girl was brought in." He paused for a moment and then added, "This little girl just died!"

Sandra Smith watched her programme on TV until 11.45 a.m., and then she got up to start lunch. Once the TV was switched off, she heard some commotion outside in the street, so she went to the front door to see what was happening. She found people staggering about on the street and vomiting; there were two people lying on the road and moaning in pain. She ran out and asked her neighbour, who was standing by her gate, "What has happened? Is this another pandemic?" Her neighbour said, "I don't know, but I think it has to be the water. My housemaid drank the water, and within fifteen minutes she felt nauseous, so I sent her to the doctor. About fifteen minutes back, people started coming out of their houses to go to the hospital, and some of them have been vomiting on the road. I have phoned everyone I know and told them not to drink the water. You drink only bottled water, I know, but did you cook with the corporation water?" Sandra said, "I've been watching TV. I was just going to start cooking when I heard the noise outside and came to see what had happened. My God! I better phone my girls and tell them not to drink any water. They've gone to their friend's house in Cheran Nagar." She ran inside and phoned her daughters, but Cheran Nagar was not affected because they did not get the water supply on that day.

12:05 P.M. TO 1:00 P.M

IT WAS A HOT SUMMER, and once again there was a scarcity of water in New Town, a sprawling suburban area of Kovai city. The district administration supplied potable water to households only once in fifteen days. The water came from the river dams and went through a series of pumping and purification stations and then into giant overhead tanks situated in different areas. From there, the water was released to specific localities on different days via a large pipe and valve network. Some of the overhead tanks were smaller and catered to a smaller locality. These were usually stand-alone tanks, unlike the larger tanks, which were enclosed by boundary walls and contained offices and generators on the premises.

The first call to the local police station was made

a few minutes past noon by the doctor of the small clinic where Divya had died. Five minutes later, they got another call, and a man shouted hysterically, “People are vomiting on the street! I just saw a man staggering out of his home, and he collapsed by the gate. Come immediately! Oh God! Is this another pandemic?” The Station House Officer spoke calmly and said, “Please, Sir, take a deep breath and just answer my questions. Where are you calling from, and what is your name?” The man took a deep breath and then spoke more calmly. “My name is Rajan,” he said. “I live alone on the fourth street in Ram Nagar. I was returning home from a trip to Chennai when I saw some people just vomiting on the streets. Nearing my home, I saw two men rolling on the ground in front of their houses, and there was a lot of loud crying and shouting from most of the houses. I ran into my home as I think that this may be another type of pandemic? I am calling you from my home. Please, please send someone to check what is happening.”

The Station House Officer, or SHO, immediately called in his people and made an announcement. “A call came in from a doctor at a local clinic who said that he had treated a child from Ram Nagar and then a family and another little girl from Anbu Nagar. Now another call has just come in from Ram Nagar, and I think it is a genuine call and not a prank because the symptoms described are somewhat the same as what the doctor told us. It seems people are vomiting in the streets and some were seen rolling on the ground in front of their houses. The caller also says that he can hear a lot of loud crying and screaming from many houses as he rushed home. Now, this may be another virus attack, or it may be something else, like an outbreak of dysentery or diarrhoea or whatever. Every one of you must wear masks and gloves, and do not touch anything with your bare hands."

He put together a team of two policemen and a policewoman headed by his Sub-Inspector and dispatched the team to Ram Nagar and Anbu Nagar. But just as the team was leaving the station, the phones started to ring. There was a switchboard that connected to three phones in the station, and all three were ringing. A policewoman who picked up one of the phones shouted out, "Sir! That was a caller from Anbu Nagar, same complaints!" Another policeman said, "Sir, this caller says the same things are happening in Vivek Nagar." The policeman who picked up the third phone said, "That was also from Ram Nagar, Sir!"

There was panic showing on the faces of some of the constables and there was a lot of softly spoken talk. The SHO was a smart and experienced man and he did not panic. His name was Gopal and he was a tall, broad-shouldered man known for his strict sense of discipline among his subordinates, but also known for his fairness and honesty. Now he spoke sternly and told his people, "We are the protectors of the public and if *we* show panic then what will the people do? Just do as I have instructed, wear your masks and gloves and do not touch anything with your bare skin. I will call in for more constables from the other area station and I will inform the city police headquarters right now!"

He made up three teams of four personnel each and assigned each of them to one of the areas. He told them, "Sub-Inspector Ramya will go with the Ram Nagar team and the other two teams will report and take orders from her. Go and assess the situation on the ground and keep in touch by phone. Let me know what the situation on the ground is as soon as you arrive at your locations. Take pictures wherever you feel it is pertinent and send them to the station. I will coordinate things from here. Go now and let us hope that this is just an outbreak of dysentery or diarrhoea!"

Sub-Inspector Ramya was a young policewoman around 24 years of age. She was five foot nine inches in height, dark-skinned, slim, and very good looking. She also held a black belt in karate. She had always wanted to join the police force from a young age, and she had passed the State Public Service

Commission examination and had been selected. She was a native of a neighbouring district and her first appointment was here in New Town. She enjoyed her work and she respected her SHO, Inspector Gopal. When she arrived with her team at Ram Nagar, she was not prepared for what she saw. Some people were running here and there in panic and she saw a man and two women lying in the street. Some people were standing in front of their houses and looking around helplessly. A few children were on the street, and three of them were rolling on the ground and crying. Everywhere she looked she could see signs of vomit, and she could hear the screaming from the houses.

She told one of her constables, "Use the loudspeaker and tell everyone to stay inside their homes and that help is on the way." She phoned the other two teams and gave them the same instructions. She then took pictures and uploaded them to the station. She told the woman constable in her team, "Keep things moving here and I'll be back in five minutes." She jumped into the police jeep and raced away to another nearby residential colony. She questioned the people there if anyone had been complaining of vomiting and stomach pain but the answer was negative. She then went to two more localities and also asked some shopkeepers on the road but all their answers were negative. No one had been complaining of vomiting or any other symptoms. She then raced back to Ram Nagar and immediately phoned the station and told Inspector Gopal, "Sir! I would recommend the immediate quarantining of these three areas. I have been to some neighbouring colonies but the symptoms seem to be confined to just these three areas! I am going to talk to some of the people now and I will get back to you."

She went to a man who was lying in a foetal position in front of a gate, and bending down she asked him, "Sir, can you tell me what is wrong? Are you in pain?" The man mumbled, "My stomach...it's killing me...my family..." He raised his hand with difficulty and pointed to the gate behind him. Ramya told the constables, "Spread out and talk to people and come and tell me what they say!" Singling out the woman constable, she told her, "Call for ambulances immediately! Tell them to wear masks and gloves but tell them they are to come immediately." She phoned Gopal again and told him, "I'm phoning for ambulances with the instruction to wear masks and gloves when they arrive, but I think you should coordinate or many of them may not come when they hear about what is happening." Gopal told her, "I'll take care of it. I'm sending constables from the neighbouring stations to bring the ambulances themselves. More constables will be arriving at the three areas to enforce quarantine within half an hour."

Ramya went to the house that the man had indicated and found the front door open. She walked in and called out in Tamil, "Anyone here? This is the police!" She heard some moaning from the next room and she went there. She found a woman sitting at the dining room table with her head in her hands and vomit spread all around her. She asked the woman in Tamil, "Big sister, can you tell me what has happened?" But the woman was disoriented and stared at Ramya without seeing her, and then she started retching again. Ramya went into the next room, which turned out to be the bedroom, and she saw a little girl of maybe three years of age lying in a bed in a pool of vomit and faeces. The room stank, but Ramya rushed to the child and felt for a pulse. There was a sadness in her eyes as she realised that the child was dead. She went out of the house and phoned Gopal again, but the lines were busy. She called him on his personal phone and he picked up immediately. She told him, "Sir! Symptoms seem to definitely be stomach pain, vomiting and diarrhoea. I just saw a little girl, maybe three or four years old, lying dead in her bedroom!"

Inspector Gopal was an empathetic man and he could hear the pain in Ramya's voice. He knew that she had lost both her parents and her four-year-old niece the previous year in a car accident, and he also knew that she had been very fond of her niece. Now he told her sternly, "Ramya! You are first a police officer and then only a woman, just as I am first a police officer and then only a man! You are the smartest person I know so get control of your emotions and go house to house and figure out how this happened. I have phoned the city crime branch and they will be arriving in a short while."

Ramya took a deep breath and then called her team. When they arrived, she told them, "Use the police van and keep taking these people to the local clinics and hospitals. Tell the hospital staff to keep them isolated for now and to be sure to wear masks and gloves. Tell them the symptoms are stomach pain, vomiting, and diarrhoea, and some people are dead already. Do not let them refuse to accept the patients! Wherever you see an ambulance, commandeer it and bring it here. If you see a van or a lorry, commandeer that also and bring them here." One of the constables asked her, "What if the drivers refuse to come?" Ramya told him, "Then tell them that they only have to drive the vehicle here and after that we will drive it. There are four of us and we can all drive, so go quickly now and do what I have said. More police will be arriving soon. I have a feeling that time is the major factor here and the sooner we get them to the hospital the better their chances will be!"

She went down the street to a house where two young boys were standing on the road and crying out for help. One of the boys shouted out to her, "Please come quickly, something is happening to mummy and daddy!" She told them to stay where they were and she went into the house. Again the stench of vomit assaulted her, but she went through the rooms until she found the couple lying on the bed. She checked for signs of life but found none. She came out and spoke to the boys. "Tell me what happened," she told them. The elder of the two said, "I don't know, the water came and mummy said that she was going to start lunch but before that, she made coffee for herself and daddy. I think about half an hour back they started to vomit and...and..." His voice trailed away and he started crying.

Ramya thought that the boy must be around ten years old and his brother maybe a year or two younger. She patted his shoulder and told him, "You are the elder son and you must be strong now. They started vomiting after they drank the coffee? Did they eat anything?" The boy stopped crying and said, "No, we all had breakfast hours ago. They complained of stomach pain about half an hour after drinking the coffee, I think..." She asked him, "Did the two of you drink any water or anything else?" He told her, “There was no water at all for two days so we drink the bottled water. From yesterday mummy was even cooking with the bottled water.”

Ramya was instantly alert and she asked him, “Do you know if she made the coffee from the bottled water or the water from the tap?” The boy was positive, “She made the coffee from the tap water.” She then asked him, “Have you any relatives or friends nearby?” The boy nodded and replied, “My cousin lives in Cheran Nagar. That is just two streets down the main road.”

She called the policewoman and told her, “Take them to their cousin's place in Cheran Nagar and tell them to keep them there. I've been there just now and no one in that area seems to be affected.” Lowering her voice she said, “Inform the adults there that both parents are dead and that we will contact them later.” After the boys left with the policewoman, Ramya phoned Gopal and told him, “I think the problem is with the drinking water supply, Sir. We should shut off the supply and inform everyone not to use the water.” Gopal said, “I told you that you were smart! The crime branch is here and the SP thinks this may be arsenic poisoning. You can tell the other teams also to inform the people about the water and I will send vans with loudspeakers as well to make announcements. We are on our way to the R.M. Hospital and if it is arsenic, then we will lift the quarantine."

Ramya phoned the other two teams and told them to inform everyone in their area not to drink the water that was supplied by the corporation. She told them, and also her team, "When you take the people to the hospitals and clinics you can tell the doctors that we suspect arsenic poisoning, but at present we are not sure. We will inform them immediately when we are sure, but for now, they should go ahead and treat the patients accordingly." One constable in her team asked her, "Madam, what if it is not arsenic poisoning? The police top brass will have your head for issuing these instructions without their permission." She told him sharply, "They can have my head if they want, but right now I have to try and save as many of these people as possible. Just do as I say, and if you are questioned later then you can say that I gave the order and so you obeyed. Go now and let's not waste time thinking about my head!"

1:00 P.M. TO 1:30 P.M

WHEN STATION HOUSE OFFICER, Inspector Gopal, phoned the city police headquarters, Superintendent of Police, or SP, Raj Kumar, of the city police crime branch, was working through some files at his office. He was sitting at his desk and he was sweating because the air conditioner was on the blink and the breeze from the pedestal fan was warm and did nothing to cool him off. The SP was a tall man, almost six feet, and well-built. His hair was starting to recede from his forehead and he was always clean-shaven. He had a face that was almost ugly looking but with character, stern and tough, and could terrify a criminal when he was angry. But whenever he smiled, his face lit up and he looked almost handsome.

Suddenly the door opened and his second in

command, Inspector Hari, charged into the room and exclaimed, "Chief! We are getting reports of multiple deaths and of hospitals and nursing homes being filled up with patients!" Raj Kumar noticed Hari's agitation and he immediately stood up and asked, "Where?" Hari replied, "Some areas of New Town. The local police station just phoned in and informed us of what is happening, but at present, they just have these bare details." Raj did not ask any more questions but just said, "Let's go!" They jumped into a car and raced away to New Town. It took them around forty minutes because of the heavy traffic on the roads and they went straight to the local police station when they reached the town. The Station House Officer, Inspector Gopal, told Raj, "People are just collapsing, some are dying, and the others are being admitted to the local nursing homes, clinics, and hospitals, which are already overflowing. My men and women are out there and they are phoning in their reports, which I am collating to try and get some sense of what is happening."

Raj asked him, "Is the whole town affected?" Inspector Gopal replied, "From what I have gathered it seems to be just three localities, Ram Nagar, Anbu Nagar, and Vivek Nagar. My Sub-Inspector Ramya is a smart woman and she took a vehicle and went racing to some of the other localities, but everything seems to be normal everywhere else except for these three areas." Raj asked him, "Population?" Gopal shrugged and said, "A lot! More than 12,000 I would say in the three localities, but that is just my estimate."

"What symptoms?" Raj asked. Gopal told him, "From what I can gather, people are vomiting, complaining of stomach pain, others are suffering from acute diarrhoea, still others are complaining of numbness of their hands and feet, cramping of their muscles and so on." Raj then asked him, "When did this start?" Gopal said, "We started getting some complaints about an hour ago, so that would be around noon? At first, it looked like an outbreak of some kind, dysentery or diarrhoea or some such infection, so we cordoned off the streets immediately where it appeared that more than a few households were affected."

Raj nodded and said, "That's good, that was a good move!" But Gopal shook his head and said, "But it didn't work, because more and more people from different streets began falling sick. Now I believe that it is confined to these three areas so we have cordoned them off, no one in and no one out." Raj put his hand on Gopal's shoulder and told him, "You did well, Inspector! It is just about an hour since you knew about this and already you have narrowed it down to these three areas and you have quarantined them. Inspector Hari and I are going to these areas and I need a local cop to guide us." Inspector Gopal said, "Take my Head Constable, Shekar, he knows everything about this town as he was born here."

Before leaving, Raj made a phone call to his brother-in-law David Joseph, and he told him, "David, I need you to come over here to New Town immediately." David said, "I know that area. I've been there before on some case-related issues." Raj said, "We were called in by the local police as it seems that people are falling ill and the symptoms that the Station House Officer just told me reminded me of arsenic poisoning!" David asked him, "Are you sure, Raj? How many people are we talking about?" Raj said, "Three areas seem to be affected according to the local Station House Officer and he estimates around 12,000 people. I just got here with Hari and I'm going now to the affected areas to see what is happening. When you get here, talk to Station House Officer Gopal and he will send you to where I am. I will be in touch with him at all times." David said, "I'll be there! But Raj, if it is arsenic and affecting an entire area then it could only be in the water supply. Get the supply shut off immediately!"

Raj told Gopal, "That was my brother-in-law, David Joseph. I need you to send some men immediately to shut off the potable water supply to all areas in the town. I need it done immediately, no delays!" Inspector Gopal shouted out to his Head Constable, Shekar, "See who is the closest to the water supply department and get them to shut down the potable water supply right now to the entire town! Whoever you send, you tell them not to take no for an answer and to get tough if the people there don't do it immediately." He then told the Writer, Shankar, "You hold down things here and keep in touch with me." He told Raj, "I am coming along with you! The Writer will coordinate things from here." But Raj said, "Before we leave, arrange for police vehicles with loudspeakers to go around all the areas, starting with these three areas you told me about. They are to announce that people should not use the potable water supplied from the corporation. Make sure that the message is clear! Do not use the water for anything, drinking, bathing, cooking, anything!" Inspector Gopal told Shekar, "You take charge of that and do it now, while I go with the crime branch officers. Just tell me where I should take them first." Head Constable Shekar told him, "I would take them to Ram Nagar as that is the largest of the three colonies." But Raj told him, "No, take us to the nearest hospital where some of these people have been admitted. It is urgent that we speak to a doctor immediately." Shekar thought for a moment and then said, "The R.M. Hospital, that is the closest and we have reports of people being admitted there."

"I know where it is," said Gopal and he went with Raj and Hari. At the door, Raj stopped and turned to Head Constable Shekar and said, "David Joseph will be coming here within an hour and he will ask for Inspector Gopal, so just send someone with him to wherever we are."

Raj, Hari, and Gopal raced to R.M. Hospital and on the way Gopal received Ramya's phone call. He told Raj what she had said and Raj told him, "I must meet this Sub-Inspector. That was very good detective work!" As soon as the car stopped, Raj was out and running into the hospital with Hari and Gopal right behind him. Raj stopped at the enquiry counter and told the lady sitting there, "I need to see whoever is in charge here. Right now!" She looked at him and then at Gopal who was in uniform and she said, "Come with me, Sir!" She took them to a nearby room and told them, "Wait here and I will call the doctor out." She went in and returned in less than a minute with a doctor who introduced himself as Dr. Ramesh. Raj told him, "I'm from the crime branch and I think that these people are suffering from arsenic poisoning. Can you do an immediate urine and blood test?" Before the doctor could respond he went on, "If you can't, then tell us which lab can do it and give me the samples. I will rush the samples there and get it done."

The doctor stared at him for a moment and then exclaimed, "Arsenic! The symptoms...yes...it could be." He told the receptionist, "Run to the lab and bring the technician here right now!" He then called a nurse and told her, "Take samples of the urine and blood from any two victims for the lab immediately!" Turning to Raj he said, "I'm sure we can do the testing right here, but arsenic?? All these people??" Raj told him, "We are thinking maybe through the corporation water supply, but we first need to get the results of the tests." The doctor agreed but then told him, "We can start treatment measures before that. I will write out what measures to take and you can make sure that every clinic and hospital gets the instructions."

He called a nurse and told her, "Start intense stomach lavage for all victims immediately and give them an intravenous drip. When you run out of equipment for the drip you can give an oral rehydration solution. Tell the pharmacy to give us all that they have and to send someone to the city to get more on an urgent basis." He then told Raj, "Besides that, we can start chelation therapy once we are sure that this is arsenic poisoning. Come, I will write out everything and you can get it circulated."

Raj looked around and then told Hari, "Just look

at this! This looks like a war zone!" There were people everywhere, sitting in every available chair and lying down on the floor as well. The nurses and attendants were running from victim to victim in a frenzy of activity. Inspector Hari was a good-looking young man around 32 years of age and was considered by the department to be Raj's protégé. He was of medium height and had a muscular body toned by daily workouts. He also held a black belt in karate and was known to be a good detective. Now he also looked around and then told Gopal, "If this is the situation in a hospital of this size, then what about the small clinics and nursing homes? They usually have only a few nurses and attendants so how will they cope with this rush?"

Gopal stared at him for a moment and then immediately took out his phone and called the station. "Remove the police personnel from quarantine duty," he told his Head Constable Shekar. "Send them to all the clinics and nursing homes and small hospitals and instruct them that they are to help the nurses and attendants in taking care of the victims. Tell them to follow whatever instructions are given by the doctors or nurses. This is urgent so deploy them within fifteen minutes! Talk to the Writer and see if he has a list of the places where the victims have been taken." He then phoned Ramya and brought her up to speed. "You can do the same thing with whatever personnel you have under your command," he told her. "Coordinate with Shekar for more personnel as needed." Ramya told him, "Sir, I've already sent some personnel to the nearby small clinics to help out. Now I will send the rest after finding out from the local people and the ambulance drivers where the victims were taken." Gopal said, "That's good Ramya, very good!" She then told him, "I am also sending the deceased victims to the government hospital in the city. Each team is keeping a record of numbers and addresses and names wherever possible of the bodies being sent to the government hospital."

While he was talking to Ramya, Raj was on the phone to city police headquarters requesting that doctors and nurses be rounded up on an urgent basis and sent to help out in the three affected areas. He told Gopal, "The Commissioner has promised to send doctors and nurses within the hour so that will bring things under some control. Now we need to go to the water department and talk to them to get some facts."

1:30 P.M. TO 2:30 P.M

GOPAL CALLED Ramya and told her, "I need you to come and meet us at the R.M. Hospital right now. You will accompany the crime branch officers and coordinate things for them. Bring a constable with you when you come. I will go back to the station as I have to coordinate with headquarters and all the clinics and hospitals where the victims have been admitted." Ramya arrived within ten minutes and after introducing her to Raj and Hari, Gopal left for the police station. Before leaving he told Raj, "She will help you with your investigations and will liaise between us for anything that you need me to do. I hope you get to the bottom of this disaster as soon as possible."

Raj, Hari, and Ramya went to the water department and met the man in charge who said his name was Muthusamy. Raj told him, "You must have heard of what has happened by now. Tell me, was water released to Ram Nagar, Vivek Nagar, and Anbu Nagar at around 11 a.m. this morning?" Muthusamy said, "Yes, we release water by rotation to different areas and today was the day for Ram Nagar, Vivek Nagar, and Anbu Nagar." Raj said, "I need you to show me the entire route that the water takes from the dam to the main overhead tank from where the water is distributed finally to these areas." Muthusamy said, "I can tell you right now that the water is not contaminated. That sometimes happens during the rainy season, but even then it is not so much contamination as just muddy water. But I will show you the entire process of where the water starts from until it reaches the overhead tanks."

Raj told him, "Let me set your mind at rest. No one is blaming you right now, because we think that a poison was somehow introduced into the water supply and we need to investigate to find out where it was done. We are waiting on some tests that are being done and then I will be able to confirm it officially." Hari was on the phone and now he told Raj, "Sir, the tests are positive for arsenic trioxide!" Raj threw up his hands and told Muthusamy, "Well! There you are, it is confirmed. You can assure me that the water supply was cut off for the entire town as soon as the police instructed you to do so?"

Muthusamy said, "Of course! No water is being supplied anywhere right now." He then opened some files on his computer and told Raj, "If you look at these drawings you can map the entire route of the water."

Raj, Hari, and Ramya together studied the drawings in detail and then Hari said, "We can test the source which is the main pumping station first, and then we can test this pumping station which seems to be right in the middle of the route. Then we can test the main overhead tank from where the water was released to these areas." Ramya said, "That's a good plan and will save time instead of testing the entire route, but why not go backwards. We first test the overhead tank which should show positive and then we check the middle pumping station. If that station is negative then we go backwards from the main overhead tank and we should find the point where the poison was introduced." Raj agreed and asked Muthusamy to send a man with them who knew the entire route that the water took.

As they were leaving the water department office, Hari asked Ramya, "How long have you been in service?" She replied, "This is my first posting and I've been here for more than a year now, a year and eight months actually." He asked her, "What's your opinion of your SHO, and don't take my question in the wrong way. The reason I am asking is simply because in a situation like this we need to know the people we can depend on. If he is not good in a crisis then we will have to bring in more of our own people and that's the reason for me asking." She gave him a steady look and said, "He is a very experienced man and I would say that he can handle any crisis." Hari said, "That's good enough for me. We just like to be sure of the people we work with." She asked him, "But are you sure about me?" He laughed and told her, "Your SHO has been singing your praises, so yes, we are sure about you!"

2:30 P.M. TO 5:00 P.M

THEY WENT from the water department to the R.M. Hospital and met the doctor. Raj told him their plan and said, "Can you send a technician with us so that he can take the water sample and bring it back to check it here at your lab?" The doctor said, "I don't mind, but aren't you supposed to get it checked at a government facility?" Raj told him, "That I will do later for official verification. Right now, I do not want to waste any time in identifying the point of entry of the poison. I will make sure that you are reimbursed for any expense or I will pay you myself, so will you help us out?" The doctor said, "Of course! I will send a man with you and I will ensure that the testing is done immediately. If the city pays me, then that's fine, but this is a disaster and I will do whatever I can to help." Raj thanked him, and they left for the main overhead tank.

When they got there, Raj saw that this was a sprawling complex of offices and generator housings all situated around a giant overhead tank placed on a network of concrete pillars and which reached up to more than thirty feet from the ground. It was a huge tank and had a capacity of two hundred thousand litres of water. Hari asked the man in charge of the distribution, “How does the water get to the tank?” The man showed him a huge underground sump and said, “The water comes here and from here it is pumped up to the overhead tank.” Hari told him, “I want a sample of the water from here and a sample of the water from the overhead tank.” He told the technician from the hospital, “Give him one container at a time and please label it correctly so that there will be no doubt later on as to where the sample was taken from.”

Just then, a police car drove up and David Joseph got down and walked over to them. He was a tall, thin, saturnine-looking man, clean-shaven, with his salt-and-pepper hair combed straight back over his head with a prominent widow’s peak. He was around 50 years of age and was quite famous as a psychological detective who had helped the police to solve a number of difficult and puzzling crimes. His sister, Priya, was married to Superintendent of

Police Raj Kumar, who was also his childhood friend from their schooldays. Raj, David, and Hari had been involved in many cases together over the years.

David walked up to them and said, "Hi Raj, Hari! So this is the place from where the water is distributed to the houses?" Raj said, "Yes, David. We mapped the route the water takes from the dam through all the pumping and purification stations, etc. to here. We are now checking the samples here and then we will check the pumping station that is in almost the centre of the route. If this is positive and that is negative, then we will work backwards from here to find the entry point of the poison." David told him, "Good thinking Raj! Smart as ever, I see, or is it Hari?" Raj told him, "Neither of us actually. It was Sub-Inspector Ramya's idea."

He introduced Ramya to David and she shook his hand solemnly and said, "*The* David Joseph! I'm honoured, sir, to shake your hand." David gave her a disarming smile and said, "Just David, please, Inspector." He looked around the place and then asked her, "Do you think that this is the entry point?" Ramya replied, "We will know that after we check the other pumping station and then work backwards from here if necessary." David regarded her for a moment and then said, "That is not my question. I am asking you if *you* think that this is the actual entry point." Ramya gave him a look of surprise and then said, "My personal opinion? Yes, I think that this is the entry point. From the middle pumping station, the water goes to many overhead tanks, but there has been no similar report of such an outbreak anywhere else up to now."

David nodded and told her, "That's what I think as well, so let's study this place and see how it is possible for someone to introduce at least fifty kilograms of arsenic trioxide powder into the water without any of these people being aware of it." Hari exclaimed, "Fifty kilograms!?" David told him, "I spoke to Vijaya and she says that it would take at least fifty to seventy kilograms of the powder in such a large quantity of water for it to have such an immediate effect. She also said that most probably it would be the last overhead tank from where the water is dispersed to the houses. She based that assumption again on the fact of the fast reactions displayed by many of the victims. She said if this was the entry point, then the potency of the poison would be greater, which is the case as we know it."

Vijaya was an expert in poisons and she was known to Raj and Hari as well. When she was in school, her fifteen-year-old friend was raped by three rich men, and they had escaped justice using their money power. Her friend never recovered fully from that trauma, and so twenty years later Vijaya poisoned and killed the three men. She had hoped that their deaths would finally bring closure for her friend. A man who had loved her friend at the time of the rape and who had still hoped to marry her, joined Vijaya, and they had executed the poisoning in such a way that the police were going around in circles trying to solve the case.

David had figured out how it was done, but he had dropped the case citing lack of evidence. The people closest to him, however, knew that he had dropped the case because he believed that justice had been done. Vijaya's friend, Vanitha, had taken part in the vigilante campaign to force the government to implement police reforms in the country, and she had died during that campaign. Vijaya had also taken part in it and she had remained close to David after the campaign ended when they had achieved their objective.

Raj called one of the workers and told him, "Open that sump, please." The man removed the manhole cover and Raj and David looked down into the deep sump. "There's not much water here," Raj said. The man said, "That's because we pumped the water to the overhead tank early this morning. The overhead tank was almost empty and only after pumping up the water could we release it to the designated areas." David asked him, "So when did the water come into this sump?" The man called his supervisor over and David repeated the question. The supervisor said, "We were told that the water would reach the sump sometime around 3 a.m. so we came in at around 7 a.m. and started pumping up the water to the overhead tank." David asked him, "So yesterday this sump was almost empty? When was the last time you released the water from the overhead tank to other areas in the town?" The man thought for a moment and then told him, "Last morning we received water here and we pumped it up and the water was distributed from the tank to four localities from the afternoon to the evening. After that, the overhead tank was almost empty and so was this sump."

Ramya was talking to the men who worked in the offices below the overhead tank and David walked over to join her. She was asking one of the men, "Tell me honestly, is it possible for someone to enter this compound without anyone seeing them?" The man pointed to the surrounding compound wall and the high gate with a lock on it and said, "When no one is here then the gate is locked. So it would be difficult for anyone to enter without being seen. As you can see, this place is in the middle of a residential colony so it is surrounded by houses." Ramya looked at the wall which was about five feet in height and then looked at the gate which was a fabricated open trellis work made of iron. She then looked at the two houses that were in front of the tank compound and asked the man, "Who lives in those two houses?" He shrugged, and one of the other men replied, "Both those houses have senior citizens who are retired. I know both the families. That house has a husband and wife in their late sixties and an elderly mother who must be in her late eighties. That other house has a couple who must be in their seventies. No children in either of the houses. The children only come on visits."

Ramya walked over to the gate with David and examined the lock. David asked her, "What do you think?" She shrugged and replied, "It will not be difficult to open this lock." David told her, "I agree, so it must have been done at night. But there is a street light right there between the two houses and that would light up the front of the gate." He called one of the men over and asked him, "Does that street light sometimes break down?" The man said, "Oh yes! Many times, but we always get it replaced the next day."

Ramya asked him, "During the night, is this place empty or does someone always come here for some work or something?" The man said, "We used to have a person living on the premises before, but not for the last one year. If someone comes here in the middle of the night, it would only be for something urgent. Maybe they need some details from the office or maybe water is being released to this sump and it has to be immediately pumped to the overhead tank. You can talk to the man who is in charge of all that." He called out, "Big brother, can you come over here?" A short man with greying hair came over and Ramya asked him the same question. He thought for a moment and then told her, "It happens, but not often. Usually, this place is closed for the night, but the lights outside the office are always on so it is never in total darkness." Ramya thanked him and he went away.

David asked her, "So now what do you think?" She said, "If someone watched this place for even a week, they would know when to enter the compound without anyone seeing them." David agreed but added, "But still there is always the risk of the unexpected." Ramya asked him, "But a terrorist is one who does not mind dying for his cause, isn't it? So they would take a chance on the unexpected." David agreed but told her, "Yes, they will die for their cause, but they do not want to get caught before carrying out their attack. There is a difference. They will plan their attack so that they can execute it without getting caught beforehand because that would defeat their purpose and then the other members would be caught as well. But during an attack, yes, they won't mind dying for their cause."

Ramya thought about that for a while and then

she remarked, "Yes, I get what you are saying, but then if this is not a terrorist attack...?" But David demurred and said, "We don't know yet if this is a terrorist attack or not. We will have to check and see just how vulnerable to unauthorised access this compound is. But in case it turns out that this is not a terrorist attack, then I would say that it is the act of an insane mind." Ramya was shocked and said, "A madman? A madman would do something like this?" David admonished her, "The way you say madman, it is obvious to me that you imagine a crazy-looking person walking along the road, talking to themselves and acting demented. That is not an insane person; that is a person suffering from dementia or sometimes acute schizophrenia. A person with an insane mind would appear quite sane to everyone, although dogmatic about his or her convictions. The line between sanity and insanity is a very thin one and an insane mind could do something like this just to prove something to themselves or to others."

Ramya was interested and said, "So you're talking about a psychopath." But David told her, "A psychopath is also insane, but the difference is that a psychopath is born that way. They are born without the basic human emotions and they just mimic those emotions when it suits them. A psychopath could do something like this just to kill one person who insulted him or her or even an imagined insult. A psychopath would not worry that to kill that one person, he or she would have to kill a hundred people. But a normal person can also become insane due to various reasons. That person would appear sane and, in fact, *would* be sane in many ways except for that one point that his or her mind gets fixated on. Then they can do something like this without any remorse for the consequences of their action."

Raj and Hari had come up by that time and Raj told Ramya, "Getting a firsthand lesson in psychology, I see!" Turning to David, he asked him, "So you are thinking that this may be the work of an insane mind? I will still have to work the terror angle and the national investigating agencies will also take over this case, I am sure." David agreed and told him, "Right now I would bet on the terrorist angle, so you work that angle and when the national agencies take over then maybe you can join us." Ramya stared at him in surprise and asked, "You will let me work with you on this?" He regarded her for a moment and then said, "You will have to do everything in your off-duty hours as this would be an unofficial investigation. It may very well turn out to be another terrorist attack and we would be wasting our time."

Her eyes lit up and she said, "Not a problem! Not

a problem at all! Not if I can work with *the*...with you." David smiled and said, "So let us go first and talk to the people in these two houses. Raj and Hari can continue with the sampling of the water here and work backwards." He told Raj, "This sample will be positive I am sure. To save time, leave the other pumping station and just take a sample from the place just before this one and if that is negative then your work is done." Hari asked him, "You are sure that this is the place, David?" David replied, "Yes, I think the powder was dumped in that underground sump. That cover is not that difficult to move, whereas climbing up to the top of that tank with fifty kilograms of the powder would be arduous, and also increases the risk of being caught. Since there were no complaints from the other areas that received water yesterday evening, then it stands to reason that the poison was dumped in this sump last night."

He thought for a moment and then remarked, "With the water gushing into the sump in the early hours of today, and then the motor being switched on to pump the water from here to the overhead tank, that poison would have mixed very well with the water instead of settling down at the bottom. No wonder the arsenic acted so swiftly. The water would have been literally laced with arsenic!" He thought for a moment and then said, "I would bet that the poison was dumped very late last night. Ramya and I are going to find out just how easy it is to gain access to this compound at night."

They walked towards the first house that was directly opposite the tank and Ramya said, "You don't seem fully convinced that this is a terrorist act. Why is that?" David was serious when he told her, "To me, any such attack is a terrorist act. A bomb being placed in a restaurant is a terror attack. A mob running wild and attacking people of one community is also a terror attack. The very term 'terror attack' means to create terror, so even this poisoning is a terror attack to me. I am only doubting whether an organised terror cell is responsible for this attack." Ramya persisted and asked him again, "And why is that?" David pondered for a moment and then told her, "We will have to check the diversity of the population in these three areas. Religious dominance or caste dominance, that will be the deciding factor, I think. I have been to this area a few times in the past, and my impression was that there is no particular dominance of any kind."

They had reached the house and David opened the gate and walked inside. They went up to the front door which was open and David rang the calling bell. A man and woman, who appeared to be senior citizens, came rushing to the door and David said, "If you don't mind, we would like to ask you a few questions." They looked at Ramya who was in uniform and the woman said, "Please come in." But David told her, "Thank you, but we can talk right here. You see, we want to ask you certain questions that pertain to that water tank." He pointed to the huge overhead tank as he spoke and the man immediately said, "You are here about that poisoning attack? We've just been on the phone with our friends and the whole town is talking about the water supply being poisoned. We have not touched the water after we heard about what had happened." David asked him, "When did you get the water supply?" The woman answered and told him, "We got the water supply about eight days ago, I think, so we have another week or so to go before our turn comes again." David told them, "Since you've been using the water for so many days there is nothing for you to fear. You can continue using the water that you have."

He looked at Ramya and she asked the couple, "I would like you to tell me everything you can about the work timings of that tank. For example, is that gate always locked during the night?" The couple looked at each other and the man said, "Well, we lock up the house by 9 o'clock every night unless our children are visiting, so I can't really say if that gate is always locked." The wife said, "But sometimes when we have to come outside or happen to look outside, I can say that the lights are always on over there." Ramya then asked the man, "Are there many people who use this road late at night?" The man shrugged and said, "As I told you, we lock up by 9 o'clock, so I can't really say. We are retired now and we tend to lock up early and watch TV and go to bed." David said, "Thanks so much for your time."

The man asked Ramya, "Is what we are hearing true? Hundreds of people have died, they say!" Ramya said, "The police will issue a press release in due course, but as of now there is no reason to panic as we have the situation under control." As they walked out the gate, Ramya asked David, "You were saying about the population diversity in the three areas?" But David told her, "We'll get into that later. Right now, let's concentrate on finding out just how vulnerable this tank compound is." They walked over to the next house and there again they met with the same response. These were also retired people and they tended to lock up early and did not know anything about whether people worked in the tank offices in the night or not.

They stood on the road and David looked at the houses lining the street on the opposite side of the tank. The tank was situated at the end of a line of houses and there was a road at the end of the compound wall. David rubbed his chin and told Ramya,

"People from any of the other houses, whether on this side or that, would not be able to identify if a person entering the compound was actually a water department personnel or a stranger. Let's take a walk around the tank and see if there is any other way to enter the compound." They walked around the compound and finally came back to the front gate. Ramya said, "So this front gate has these two houses opposite but they lock up early. That side of the compound abuts the wall of a house, but the wall is high on that side so the people there cannot see into the compound even if they were awake and looking out. On the other hand, no one can climb over the wall on that side. The other side of the compound abuts the road, and again, with the wall being of a height of five feet no one can really see inside the compound. But again, there is a street light there and also there are houses facing that road so anyone climbing that part of the compound wall would be easily seen from those houses. At the back of the compound there are again houses, but the offices in the compound are built against the back and side walls and so they block the view of anyone from those houses. And of course, as before, no one can climb that part of the wall because it abuts the houses there. I think if an entry was made, then it had to have been made from here."

David agreed and then said, "To be sure, we will

ask Gopal for permission and we will come here in the night and see if it is really that simple to enter the compound. How good are you at picking a lock?" Ramya told him, "That lock I can certainly pick! How fast I can do it? I will have to try to know."

5:00 P.M. TO MIDNIGHT

THEY WENT BACK to the police station and joined Raj and Hari. Raj told David, "The samples here are positive. We checked the sump that is located before this one and we will be getting those results any time now. The central investigating agencies will be here tomorrow and they will be taking over the case. The Chief Minister's office has asked us to liaise with them and provide them with whatever help or logistics they may require. Hari and I have been deputed to be the liaisons and to work the case with the central agencies. I have asked for Gopal and Ramya to be deputed temporarily to the crime branch and it has been approved, so they will be working with us on this case." David said, "That's good to know, so can I appropriate Ramya to help me roam around and do some digging of my own?"

Hari smiled at Ramya and told her, “It’s always a pleasure to work with David, but be warned! Once he sent me into a psychopath’s house to search for evidence, and what I found was a house of horrors!” David said mildly, “Don’t listen to him, Ramya, he actually enjoys walking into danger. Besides, I only made the suggestion and Raj chose Hari as the person to enter that house.” Ramya said, “Yes, I know about that case! It made the headlines and Superintendent of Police Raj and Inspector Hari became quite famous.” Hari shrugged and told her, “At that time I was a Sub-Inspector and Raj was an Inspector.”

David said, “I want to talk to Gopal.” They all walked into Gopal’s office and David told him that he and Ramya planned to see just how easily a person could enter the tank compound that night. Ramya said, “I can place a constable on both ends of the road so that if anyone sees us trying to break into the compound they won’t panic when they see the constables in uniform. I don’t want to create another panic situation!” David said, “They won’t be visible to anyone from the houses, but they will be there just in case. They won’t stop anyone who uses the road either, as that would defeat our purpose. Ramya just wants them there in case anyone sees us and raises an alarm. Of course, if an alarm is raised then it means that entry into the compound is not that easy."

Hari told him, "But people will now be vigilant and more curious because of what happened today. Before this, I am sure that no one bothered about who entered the compound." David said, "I agree, but if today we are able to enter without raising an alarm, then it will only underline how easy it must have been for the perpetrator." Ramya asked David, "So at what time are we planning on doing this?" David told her, "The witching hour! We will go there at midnight."

Gopal agreed with everything and told them, "I am talking to the water department because they have to plan about cleaning out the sump and the tank and washing out all the pipes as well. Just imagine the waste of water and that too during this hot summer when there is already water scarcity!" Raj was on the phone and he now told them, "The other sample is negative, so the powder was dumped in the sump. At least the cleaning up will therefore be more confined now."

Ramya asked Gopal, "Sir, any information on how many fatalities and how many people were affected?" Gopal said sombrely, "So far the death toll is being put at 48, and the number of people who fell ill is still being tabulated, but the number is definitely more than 500. It's a wonder that more people weren't affected and that more did not die." David told him, "I think that is because people put two and two together very fast and figured out that the water was contaminated and so people simply stopped using the water. Ramya figured it out very fast and the announcements over the police loudspeakers did the rest. Raj thinking about arsenic sped up the process of treatment, and supplying all the clinics and nursing homes with that doctor's instructions on treatment really helped. I admire the speed with which this police station tackled the emergency. You are to be commended!" Raj remarked, "I will be sending in my report and you can bet that they will be commended!"

At midnight, David and Ramya walked casually down the road where the tank was located. They were dressed in khaki-coloured clothing because David had noticed that most of the tank personnel dressed in khaki. They reached the gate, which was locked, and Ramya took out two slim metal implements from her pocket and after probing the lock for less than a minute she opened it. David noticed that all the houses were in darkness except for a few night lights here and there. They opened the gate and walked inside and went and sat on the sump for ten minutes. Ramya told David, "This is too easy! We should have *some* security for our main water supply. Anyone can come in here and contaminate the water and no one would know anything about it." David agreed and said, "We concentrate on providing security to religious and other places where the government thinks a terrorist attack could take place, but no one really thinks about a simple thing like the main water supply."

Ramya was quite agitated and she said, "But someone must have said something about this at some time or the other. Now that it has happened it is so obvious to me that the danger is real. At least from now on I am sure that the security will be tightened at such places. Entry to such places should be strictly controlled in the future." David had been rubbing his chin, which was a mannerism of his when he was thinking deeply, but now he suddenly looked at her and asked, "What was that you just said?" Ramya frowned and said, "I was saying that the entry to such..." But David cut her off and said, "No, no, before that! Someone must have said something?" She said, "Oh! I said that at some time or the other I'm sure someone must have said something about the security of such places. But as usual I guess no one really listened!"

David's eyes had lit up and he murmured, "Well, that's a good starting point I think!" Ramya frowned again and asked him, "What's a good starting point?" But David looked at his watch and stood up saying, "Well, that's more than ten minutes, so let's go now." They left after relocking the gate and went home. David told Ramya that he was staying at his sister's place since it was closer than his own home. "Give me a call in the morning when you're ready and we'll meet at the police station," he told her.

THE FIRST ATTACK

MAY 13, THURSDAY – 11:50 P.M.

THE MAN

THE MAN WAS exultant at what he had achieved. He had planned well, and although it had taken time, he was now ready. He would show everyone! *'Now,' he thought, 'let us see what the reaction will be.Those poor Dalits. People just didn't care, they only preached.'* They acted as though they were taking security seriously after that incident but he knew it was only talk. Well, now he would prove it! On the table were two containers which each held twenty-four kilograms of the powder. He had done his research and he had painstakingly accumulated the powder a little at a time over a three-month period. *'Yes,' he thought, 'it had taken time, but it was foolproof! No one would be able to trace the powder back to him.'* Not even the break-in at the factory which had netted him most of the powder in one night. He dressed in khaki-coloured clothing and put on a surgical mask and a peaked cloth cap. People wearing surgical masks had become so common during the pandemic that nobody noticed it anymore. He then picked up one of the two containers and went outside to his scooter.

His scooter was an electric one and it ran silently. He had splashed mud over the licence plates so that no one would be able to read the numbers correctly. Placing the container on the footboard below his seat, he went back and returned with the second container. He placed that also on the footboard and then started the scooter and drove away. He made sure to drive at a normal speed until he reached his destination. He parked his scooter before the locked double gates and got down. He glanced around casually and then looked inside the compound through the bars of the gate. He had driven past the compound on different days at this same time and he knew that no one would be there, and today was no different as the compound was empty. He took two implements from his pocket and picked the lock on the gate. It took him just thirty seconds to pick the lock and then he pushed one of the gates open.

Getting on to his scooter again he drove it inside

the compound and parked it next to a large underground sump. He shut the gate and then put on a pair of skin-tight gloves and took out a large piece of cloth from his scooter and made a pad of it. Placing the cloth pad on the cement covering of the sump, he carefully slid the manhole cover onto the cloth pad so that it made no noise. He then quickly took the two containers one by one and emptied the powder into the sump. He replaced the cover carefully, again without making any loud sound, and then got on to his scooter and drove out of the gate. He closed the gate and locked it and then drove away. The time was exactly 12.05 a.m. on Friday, May 14.

INVESTIGATIONS

MAY 15, SATURDAY

DAVID AND RAMYA

THE NEXT MORNING David and Raj walked into the police station and met with Hari, Gopal, and Ramya. David told them, “It was very simple after all. We just walked in and walked out and no one was the wiser. So this could very well be a terrorist attack and you need to pursue that angle as swiftly as possible.” Raj asked him, “So since you’re sure now that this is a terror attack, you won’t be needing Ramya?” But David said, “I am still going to dig around a bit and look into some things that have occurred to me, so I would like to keep Ramya to help me out.” Raj stared at him for a long moment and then shrugged, “Close-mouthed as ever! Age doesn’t change you! Keep Ramya, but also keep me updated if you come across anything else." David said indignantly, "That's what I always do!" Raj rolled his eyes and Hari laughed and said, "Come on, David, you love the final, what is that word? Denouement!" David shrugged and muttered, "I just like to be sure of something before saying anything. And it's good to see that your wife is improving your erudition!" Hari had married David's elder stepdaughter, Devika, who was a voracious reader and had a large collection of books. David turned to Ramya and said, "Come on, let's leave these people to their investigations."

Ramya asked Gopal, "Sir, how are they going to clean out the tank and pipes?" Gopal frowned and said, "Well, I don't really know. I guess they'll just open the main pipe from the tank?" David gave Ramya a look of respect and said, "I like the fact that you're always thinking." Turning to Gopal he told him, "Contact the water department and tell them that they will have to collect all the water from the tank and the pipes in water tankers. They will then have to take the water to some place where they can purify or rather extract the arsenic from the water. If they can do that then they can use the water again. If not, then they will have to dispose of the water in some other way. Tell them to contact the pollution control board, or better yet, you can contact the board and ask them how they are going to proceed."

Inspector Gopal asked him, "I don't get it, isn't it better to just let that water go to waste? It would be faster as well." But Ramya said, "Sir, if the water is just let out of the tank, then the arsenic will pollute the ground and eventually it will get into the underground water. That's a lot of arsenic if David is right and *fifty* kilos were used to contaminate the water!" Gopal stared at her for a moment and then said seriously, "I'll do that. Just make sure that when you and David finish your investigations, you come back and don't leave the police force. We need people like you, and I will predict that you won't remain as a Sub-Inspector for long!"

David and Ramya went to Raj's house. David told her, "Raj and my sister have given me a room in their home which we can use as a base. Come in and let's sit and plan what we are going to do." David's sister Priya opened the front door and was introduced to Ramya. Priya was about 5 feet 5 inches tall, slim and good looking, and always with a fashionable hairstyle. "I've been hearing Raj and David sing your praises last night," she told Ramya. She laughed when Ramya looked embarrassed and told her, "You should be proud, because it takes a lot for these two to praise anyone. That makes you a very smart woman and you should be proud of that." David said, "Enough, Priya, let the girl be! Stop embarrassing her." They went into a well-furnished room which had a table with two laptops, letter pads and pens, and a small fridge in the corner. When they were seated Priya said, “I’ll get you guys some coffee now. If there’s anything you need later on just call me. The fridge has some snacks and cool drinks so help yourselves, please.”

While they were drinking coffee, David told Ramya, “There are two things that we need to do. First, I want to find out the demography of these three areas; how many people of different religions and how many people of all the different castes live there. You would know about that incident of human faeces being found in the overhead tank of that Dalit village...” Ramya interrupted and exclaimed, “Yes, that’s it! That’s what I was thinking about last night when I said that someone would have said something about this before.” David smiled and said, “Yes, when you mentioned that, I knew what had triggered the thought. That was good intuition again, because that’s the place to start.”

But Ramya said, “Nothing was proven in that case. I guess too much time had elapsed and they haven’t caught the criminal who did that heinous thing.” David agreed but said, “What I meant was that we start with all the talk that surrounded that incident. People would have spoken about the vulnerability of such places and I want to know who those people were." Ramya asked him, "Okay, and the second thing?"David looked confused for a moment and then smiled and said, "That was actually the second thing! The first is that we figure out the demography of these three areas. In that previous incident, that tank was contaminated because the majority in that village were Dalits so obviously they were the target. Over here, if this is a terror attack, then who was the target? Christians, Muslims, Hindus, or some caste category?"

Ramya nodded and said, "I get it, a terror attack has to attack some community or other for some stupid cause I guess. But what if there is no real dominant community in the three areas? Hindus of course will turn out to be the dominant community so maybe they were the target of the attack?" But David disagreed and told her, "Not if there are significant numbers from other communities as well. That is not how terrorism works. Terrorists choose specific targets to send a message. So if they were targeting Hindus, for example, then the message is lost if a lot of members of other religions also die in the same attack. For example, what if most Hindus by luck or chance did not use the water before the alarm was raised, but most of the other communities did. Then the message of the terrorist is lost and religious terrorism doesn't work that way. Hence the need for us to find out what the demographics of these areas show." Ramya asked him, "And if there are significant numbers of all communities living in these areas?" David shrugged and said, "Then I would start thinking of an insane mind!"

Together, they worked out a plan to figure out the demographics of the target areas. David said, "Obviously, we cannot go door to door and ask people what their religion or caste is. Census data might be of use, but accessing that data and then culling what we need from such a vast database would consume a lot of time that we don't have." Ramya was thinking as he was talking and now she said, "Maybe we can go to the local property tax office and get the records of the ownership of these properties. If I remember correctly, most of these houses have their owners living in them and very few are rented out. We could also try the electricity board and check the names on the connections."

David stared at her and then said, "You continue to surprise me! That would indeed be the best and easiest way to find the data that we want. We don't need to get to a hundred per cent because even seventy-five per cent would give us what we need." Ramya was still thinking and did not respond to the praise. After a while, she said, "Collating the data would be tedious and we would need a staff of at least twenty people if we want to get results within a week. I could instead take a laptop to my friend and she would give me software that would do the work in minutes. We could ask the departments to let us download the data or copy-paste the data onto my laptop and then the software would do the rest." David told her, "That *is* a brilliant idea! The departments, of course, would be concerned about privacy issues, but we could tell them that they could supervise what we are doing and when we are done they can make sure that everything is deleted from the laptop. That should keep them happy, I think."

Ramya asked him, "You said something about not having enough time. Are you thinking that there could be a second attack?" David was silent for a while and then he told her, "If this was a terror attack, then it is doubtful if there will be another because now the investigating agencies will be cracking down hard on every suspect and they will be all over this town. Unless, of course, the terrorists have already planned the second attack in advance and have everything in place even now. If that is the case, then there is nothing that we can do about it. But I very much doubt if that is the case, because any suspicious movement will be noted by the agencies now and they will pounce hard on anyone who behaves suspiciously. Usually, if a terrorist is planning two attacks then the second one would take place very shortly after the first one. That is the only way that they can complete their task and make their getaway." Ramya was silent so David continued, "But, if this is the work of an insane mind..." Now Ramya said, "Then this success would make him or her want to strike again?"

David was rubbing his chin and he said, "Let us think this thing through logically. A person with an insane mind would still have a logical reason for what he does. So what was the reason for this attack? You gave me the idea, the lack of security where the water supply is concerned. And when did that come to prominence? The attack on the Dalit colony! So, let us say that this person wants to prove to everyone that the water supply needs to be guarded or else it makes it easy for a terrorist to strike. How does that sound so far?" Ramya thought about it and then said, "But the incident in the Dalit village had already highlighted the problem and the officials had said that they would take measures to ensure that such things do not happen again. So that cannot be what this person wants to prove." David told her, "I like the way you think and I should tell you now that I will be recommending to Raj that he gets you transferred to the crime branch. They need people who think like you. Of course, that is if you don't have any objection to joining the crime branch!"

Ramya stared at him in surprise and then exclaimed, "Are you kidding?! I would love to join the crime branch!" Then suddenly realising who she was talking to, she said, "I'm sorry, Sir! I guess I got carried away with the thought of joining the crime branch." But David smiled at her and said, "Don't apologise, Ramya, and it's David and not Sir. Unless you feel comfortable in my presence, your mind won't work the way it should. So just continue as you were and don't change now." Then he turned serious and said, "I agree that this attack cannot be to show that the water supply can be contaminated as that has already been done in the case of the Dalit village. So what is the reason?"

Ramya said hesitantly, "Well...this person used arsenic...therefore, was the intention to cause death?" David replied, "Without doubt the intention was to cause the maximum number of deaths. This person went to the trouble of procuring more than fifty kilos of arsenic trioxide, don't forget!" Ramya nodded and went on, "So, if the intention was to cause the maximum number of deaths, then that is the same as a terror attack..." Her voice trailed away but David remained silent and waited for her to think. Suddenly she said, "That means that this person wanted to prove how easily a terrorist could attack us without the same old method of planting bombs or randomly shooting people at mass gatherings!"

David gently clapped his hands together and

said, "You are definitely crime branch material!" Ramya stared at him for a long moment and then exclaimed, "You have already figured all this out! You were just testing me to see if I could work it out by myself!" David shrugged and said, "When I recommend someone for the crime branch, that person is always very good. So yes, I have been testing you since we met and you have surpassed my expectations."

Ramya said, "Thanks, David, but where do we go from here? So this person wanted to prove that a terrorist could use our water supply to attack us and he or she has done that. So now what?" But David told her, "That is one reason, but don't forget that this could also be a revenge attack for what happened in that Dalit village." Ramya asked him, "But why attack here so far from that village?" David shrugged and replied, "This person could be angry that the police have not yet caught that culprit. He could believe that the police are not trying hard enough just because it was a Dalit village. So he could have staged this attack to prove that when people other than Dalits are affected then the police act very swiftly." He paused and then added, "Which would also mean that this person is a local."

Ramya asked him, "You keep saying 'he' so does that mean that you think a man committed this atrocity?" David frowned and said, "I actually wasn't aware of saying that. But I suppose that at the back of my mind I do think that a man is responsible for this. One factor is the weight of the powder, for example, although many a woman can lift more than that weight. Then there is the procuring of the powder. That can be done quite simply by buying small quantities from different factories in different places. A lone woman travelling to a factory outside of her place of residence and trying to buy arsenic would raise eyebrows in this country. A man can get away with it by getting friendly with the factory owner, maybe take him out for a drink, and pretend that he is going into the same manufacturing process and that he wants to do a trial run first; or something on those lines. So yes, I suppose I do think that this person is a man."

Ramya said, "I agree, but getting back to your fears of a second attack. This person obviously cannot do the same thing twice because now all the water supply routes are under tight security." David said grimly, "And that is what worries me!" He suddenly shook his head and told her, "But we are getting ahead of ourselves and that just won't do in such cases. Let us first confirm through the demographics that we are at least on the right track. Go to your friend and get that software installed and I will go and speak to Raj about getting us permission to do what we have planned."

Ramya was a bit doubtful and she said, "I doubt if even a Superintendent of Police of the crime branch can cut through all the red tape to get both departments to cooperate with us on this. It would take days if not weeks!" But David stood up and said, "Maybe not, but the Chief Minister certainly can! You go and do your stuff and I will get us the necessary permission. Let's plan on doing this tomorrow." They told Priya that they were leaving and as they were walking out the front door Ramya said with a bit of awe in her voice, "You can get the Chief Minister to...but of *course*, after all, you are *the*..." But David just held up his hand and she smiled and fell silent.

David went to Raj's office and told him what he had planned to do. Raj said, "It would take time to convince these two departments to cooperate, but you know that, so what is it that you really want me to do?" David said, "Talk to the Director General of Police and tell him what I said. Ask him to get me a meeting or even a phone call with the Chief Minister." Raj immediately put through a call and within five minutes he was talking to the Director General of Police. After he spoke, he held out the phone to David and said, "He wants to talk to you." David took the phone and said, "Yes, Devendra, I think this is important." The DGP said, "David, are you saying that this is not the work of a terrorist organisation?"

But David told him, "Let the investigating agencies pursue that line, and they can do that better than I can anyway. But just in case I am right and this is the work of a single individual with a twisted mind, then I need to find this person."

The DGP was silent for a while and then he said, "Stay right there and I will call you back in half an hour!" Within half an hour the Director General of Police called back and told David, "Raj will coordinate with the departments as the Chief Minister's liaison. The Chief Secretary will do the needful today and you can go to the departments tomorrow morning with Raj and get your work done. The Chief Minister told me to tell you that he hopes you are wrong this time. He said, and I quote, 'We can track down and eliminate a terrorist cell, but if this is a lone psycho then who knows what more will happen.' I wish you luck, David."

When Ramya came back after seeing her friend, David told her what had happened and then said, "Since we have the rest of the day, let's look into who said what around the time of the incident at the Dalit village. How do you propose that we go about doing that?" Ramya had a delighted look on her face when she told him, "I thought you would want to move fast on this, so I got my friend to install two pieces of software on my laptop. One is for the data that we will download tomorrow and one is a search engine that we can use to find whatever was said on television at the time of that incident!"David was curious and he asked her, "Before joining the police force, what did you graduate in at college?" She immediately said, "Computers of course!" David smiled and said, "Of course!"

They went to their room at Raj's house and Ramya opened the search program and asked David, "What keywords do you want to use?" David thought for a moment and then said, "Let's use Dalit...no, that would give us too much to check. Let's use faeces, overhead tank, contaminate, and security at first. Then we will use the word terror or terrorist to search those results and let's see what we will find." It took about fifteen minutes for the first search to be over and Ramya said, "That's a whole lot of data! It looks like every television channel was talking a lot about that incident. But now I will run the second word on this data and let's see what we get." The second search was over in a few minutes and Ramya said, "Okay, that's not much, so let's see what we've got."

There were four interviews on television studios and they watched all four. Three of the interviews featured a Dalit social activist named Hariharan, and he was very vocal and very angry for the greater part of the interviews. He was a tough-looking man, dark-skinned, with close-cropped hair, and David described his eyes as 'wild-looking.' In one of the interviews he told the television anchor, "I would like to see if this same thing happens in a village or town with upper castes and not Dalits what the official reaction would be!" The anchor said, "Well, the official reaction even here has been one of outrage and they have moved fast to try and find the culprits." The activist almost shouted, "The reaction of outrage is a political one! You say that they have moved fast? Well they haven't, because that's the reason why I doubt if the culprit will ever be caught." On another channel the activist said pretty much the same things, but then he said, "There is a sense among us Dalits that people are expressing outrage, but what are they thinking internally? Are they thinking, well it's only a Dalit village, let's just hope the same thing doesn't happen to us!"

Before the anchor could respond he said, "I know, I know, politically incorrect to say such things, but I wonder, if I had the ability to look into a person's mind and read their thoughts, I wonder what I would find!" The anchor said, "I don't think the majority of people think like that nowadays. I will admit that caste feeling and discrimination are still there, but not to the extent that it was in the past." The activist then said, "You know, now that it has been proven just how easily the water supply can be contaminated, the people in power should start thinking of tighter security. What if some terrorist contaminates the main water supply? What will happen then?" The anchor said, "I'm sure that the government is aware of that and that they are taking measures to safeguard the water supply." The activist said, "Well, we'll just have to wait and see, won't we!"

The only other interview was on an English news channel and the anchor was talking to a writer. The anchor introduced the writer as Mr Siva, the author of two books. The anchor asked him, "You've written in one of your books that it is wrong for the government and the police to just be on the lookout for bombs and guns where terrorists are concerned. You say that there are so many other ways that a terrorist can strike, and you have actually cited the city water supply as one of the dangers. Do you feel that this incident provides proof for what you've written?" The writer was a lean, fair-skinned man, with slightly long hair. He had a pleasant face with slightly deep-set, intense-looking eyes. He gave the anchor a rueful smile and said, "When I wrote that book people said that such things just don't happen. They said it wasn't that easy to contaminate the drinking water supply. Some asked me why I thought that terrorists would do such a thing. After all, they said, terrorists don't really attack everyone at the same time, they always have specific targets!"

The anchor said, "Well, in this case also, a Dalit village was the specific target as that small overhead tank catered only to that village." The writer shifted in his seat and said irritably, "But just see how easily it was done! The same thing can happen on a larger scale and then what! Will people only open their eyes after disaster strikes and not before?" The anchor was conciliatory and said, "Of course, of course, no one is saying that it cannot happen. I guess what people are saying is that so far terror attacks have always had specific targets. Let me also qualify that by saying, 'in this country at least.' There have been terror outfits worldwide that have carried out attacks just to create terror and there were no specific target communities or anything like that." Siva said, "So you are saying that we must wait until such an attack happens over here and then we will all sit up and take notice!"

The anchor told him, "No, I am not saying that. The water department officials have promised to look into the issue of safety and security where our water supply is concerned and I'm sure that they will do that. I very much doubt if such a thing will happen again." Siva was agitated and said, "All of you are the same! You wear blinkers and just refuse to see what can happen. When it does happen then it will be too late to remove your blinkers, and that is the saddest part of it all." The anchor said, "I see that besides the water supply you have also outlined other ways that a terror attack could happen. By air? You mean by drones?" Siva said, "There are many ways by which that can happen." The anchor said, "But the authorities have already cracked down on drones, so I'm sure that won't be feasible." Siva sat back in his chair with a resigned smile on his face and he said, "Well, I won't argue with you. I guess we will wait until something happens and only then will we respond. As usual!"

Ramya said, "Well, those are the only two who used the word terror. Do you want to watch all the other interviews as well?" David was thoughtful when he said, "Let me watch these interviews again." After they had run through the interviews a second time, David told her, "I think we will start with these two for the moment. Let's check where they live and see if we can find out where they were on the night that the arsenic was put in the sump." He rubbed his chin and then said, "Also let's check with the police about their investigations into the sale of arsenic trioxide." Ramya said, "We walked down the road to the tank compound last night, but how did the perpetrator get there? He must have used a vehicle to transport the fifty kilograms of arsenic." David stared at her and then said, "Go on, let's hear the rest."

"Well," Ramya continued. "I'm just thinking, a motorbike may not be suitable because of the noise, so maybe a scooter or a moped? But even a scooter or a moped makes some noise, and since it would have been around midnight..." David said, "You're thinking an electric vehicle. Yes, it could very well be, since the perpetrator would not want to attract any attention due to the noise of the vehicle." He rubbed his chin and after a while he said, "I think you're onto something. Even if people are not bothered to look at what is happening at the tank, yet, if you're by your window or your door and you hear a vehicle passing by, you usually tend to look out. People might remember seeing a vehicle so late at night on any road leading to the tank, especially after the disaster happened. The perpetrator would not want that, so yes, I think you're right. Let's keep it in mind that an electric vehicle may have been used."

Ramya started to say something but David raised his hand to cut her off and she remained silent. David was rubbing his chin and he seemed to be thinking deeply. It was obvious to Ramya that while his eyes were looking at her he wasn't really seeing her. After a while he sighed and his eyes focused on her. He told her, "I always say that the worst thing that a detective can do is to jump to conclusions too early in a case. I think that I have been doing exactly that right now!" Ramya was puzzled and she asked him, "I don't understand, how do you mean that you are jumping to conclusions?" He said, "I have picked on these two people based on their use of the word terror, and so I have ignored the rest of the debates and interviews regarding the Dalit incident. That is jumping to a premature conclusion. I have to listen to all the debates on the subject."

Ramya was still puzzled and she asked him, "But the hypothesis is that this person would bring in the issue of a terror attack. Isn't that the reason why we have culled all the data?" David agreed but explained, "You can talk about the same thing without using the words terror or terrorist. You can talk about a mass killing or a mass random public attack and it would mean the same thing." She stared at him for a long moment but then just said, "Well, let's get started because that will take us the rest of the day to complete!"

They split up the debates and interviews between themselves and got down to watching and listening. Each of them had a laptop and headphones so that they wouldn't disturb each other. David had told her, "Let's watch, listen, and make notes and we can discuss what we find once we have finished going through everything." It took them nearly five hours and it was nearly 10 p.m. when they finally finished going through all the footage. Then they sat together and compared notes, and whenever one of them wanted to see a particular footage a second time they would do so on Ramya's laptop using the search engine.

Ramya's list included an environmental activist named Swarna who said, "This same modus operandi could be used for a mass event or a mass killing and that is what scares me. Imagine if instead of faeces a person dumps something like an insecticide into the water supply!" To which the television anchor had said, "But surely only a lunatic or a psychopath would want to do something like that?" Swarna asked her, "Are you telling me that we don't have psychopaths in our country? Our natural resources and our environment are so precious and necessary for our very survival and yet we tend to ignore it rather than protect it!"

Another interview that Ramya had culled was with a political analyst called Rajesh. He had said, "You know, to me this has set a dangerous precedent. Something on these lines could be used to trigger a mass outbreak in an attempt to discredit the government. An event like this could give people bad ideas." The anchor had said, "But how would the government be discredited if some lunatic decides to kill a lot of people?" Rajesh said, "Because security is the business of the government. Of course, only a lunatic with extreme political views would even think of something so outrageous!"

David had culled an interview with another social activist named Faisal Ahmed who worked for the upliftment of the socially deprived sections of society. He was categorical and blunt when he stated, "Simply put, something like this can be used to carry out mass killings of the general public. Just think for a moment, what if a poison had been dumped into the overhead tank, and what if the overhead tank was one of the large ones that supply water to a very large area, what then? Can you imagine the havoc, can you imagine the number of people who would be affected, the number of fatalities?" The anchor said, "Well, after this incident I am sure that the authorities will tighten security over the water supply routes."

Faisal shrugged and said, "Let's hope that what you have just said is true and the authorities will take security very seriously." The anchor said, "I'm sure they are taking this seriously." Faisal told her, "As I said, I hope you're right, but look at what the past shows us. Change has only ever happened after something drastic takes place. Is this incident drastic enough for a change of attitude towards the downtrodden? I doubt it! But if this were to happen on a mass scale, then I'm sure that change would take place." He paused for a reflective moment and then said, "But what a price to pay for change!"

David said, "There are one or two more like that, but it's late so let's call it a day." He looked at the time and said wryly, "Or night, since it's almost 11 p.m. now!" Ramya asked him, "What are you going to do with what we have culled out of the footage?" David said, "Well, I will need to talk to these people so that I can evaluate their emotional state of mind. But we'll figure that out later. Tomorrow we go to the water and electricity departments and we'll try to get a sense of the demographics of these three areas."

He walked her to the front door and they met Raj who had just come in from work. "How are things going with the central investigating agencies?" David asked him. Raj shrugged and replied, "Well, they made a list of all the suspects that they have been keeping an eye on and they started their raids immediately. They've raided about four locations so far and have taken in some people for questioning. They have also sent teams to question some people who are in jail pending their trial." Ramya said, "But so far those are all people who are suspected of being involved in making bombs and buying firearms. Do they think that they can get some input from them on something like this?"

Raj told her, “Well, they’re hoping that there would have been some chatter among such extreme groups, and they’re hoping that they can get a lead if it emerges that there were rumours of an impending attack of this type.” David said, “The problem with that method is that when these people are promised some leniency if they come up with a lead, then the tendency is for them to come up with an imaginary one.” Raj shrugged again and said, “I know, I know, but I don’t blame the agencies for trying. There is absolutely nothing to go on in this case. We are still trying to trace the sale of arsenic trioxide but that is going to take a long time. Other than that we have nothing, no fingerprints, no sighting of a suspicious character, absolutely nothing at all. What about you guys, what have you been doing?” David said, “We’ll discuss that later after we go to the departments tomorrow. Let me first set my mind at rest regarding the demographics of the areas involved.”

Ramya left to go home and David and Raj sat down for a late dinner with Priya. During the course of the meal Raj remarked, “David seems to be very taken up with Ramya. She is very intelligent of course, but it’s been a long time since I’ve seen David take on a protégé and to me I think that is what he is doing now.” Priya told him, “Raj, you’re a very intelligent man, but at times you can be quite obtuse! Ramya reminds him of Revathi and we all know that Revathi is his favourite stepdaughter." Raj looked a bit confused and said, "But there's no similarity between the two! Revathi is much shorter..." But Priya cut him off and said, "The similarity is not physical Raj. They are both tough and intelligent young women and David keeps pushing her to think and reason just like he used to do with Revathi. Even *he* may not realise it but I do." David frowned at both of them and said, "Just on the off chance that the two of you imagine I'm not here, let me tell you that I *am* here so stop dissecting me!" Raj and Priya both laughed, but David suddenly realised that his sister Priya was right; Ramya did remind him of Revathi!

It was David's habit to call his wife, Rani, every night when he was away from home on some case. The previous night he had not called her since he had been busy until well past midnight. Now he called her and told her everything that had happened. "So you think that this isn't the work of a terrorist?" Rani asked him. David said, "It's early days yet, but yes, that's the way I'm starting to think now." They spoke some more and Rani told him to be careful and to come back home as soon as possible.

DATA

MAY 16, SUNDAY

RAJ, David, and Ramya went first to the Electricity Department at around 10 a.m. on Sunday morning. Raj told them, "This being a Sunday, most of the personnel are on their weekly off, but the Superintendent will be here with someone who knows how to get us what we need." They were met by the Superintending Engineer, who introduced himself and his colleagues. "My name is Samuel," he told them. "This man is Loganathan, and this guy here is Jagan, who is in charge of maintaining our records. Loganathan is our computer guy, so I asked him to come in, even though it's a Sunday, and he readily agreed to do so." Loganathan said with a small smile, "Yeah, I readily agreed after he told me that the Chief Minister would have my job if I didn't come in!"

Raj introduced David and Ramya, and Loganathan said, "Now I'm glad that I came in! At least I can say that I met and spoke to David Joseph!" David smiled and told him, "Well, now that we have all been introduced, why don't you and Jagan sit down with Sub-Inspector Ramya and she will tell you what she wants." Samuel said, "Yes, let's get this done as soon as possible. You guys work on that while the SP, David, and I work on getting some coffee and snacks for you guys."

It took them about three hours to complete the task and Ramya told David, "I think that's all we can get from here. After we get the data from the property tax office, I will collate the two and then we will get some idea of what we are looking for. Nathan has agreed to come with us and help out. He's a genius if you ask me! We wouldn't have finished so soon if not for him." David smiled and said, "Coming from you I guess that's high praise indeed!" Accompanied by Loganathan, they then went to the property tax office where again they were met by the man in charge with two of his aides and they got down to work. This time it took nearly four hours before Ramya pronounced herself satisfied. When they were leaving the office, Ramya told David, "Nathan has offered to come with us and help with the collating of details using the software my friend gave me."

David asked him, "This is your day off and we have already given you so much to do. Are you sure you want to come and help us again? I don't think the department will pay you for this overtime!" Loganathan shrugged and said, "That's okay, I've got no plans for today anyway. Besides, that software intrigues me and I would like to run it fully and see its capabilities." He was a good-looking tall young man with close-cropped hair and now he turned and smiled at Ramya, who smiled back at him. Raj and David followed them out of the office and Raj whispered to David, "I wonder if it's the software or Ramya that intrigues him!" David said with a small smile, "Well, she already calls him Nathan!"

They sat in the room at Raj's house, and while Ramya and Nathan went through the data they had collected, David sat with his headphones on and listened again to the television footage. After about two hours Ramya stood up and said, "I think that is the best that we can do." David took off his headphones and asked her, "So what did you find?" She told him, "From what we can gather going by names, there is a sizeable number of religious minorities in the three areas. Caste-wise data is harder to figure out, but again, going by names I would say that there is no real dominant community, other than if you take Hindus as a whole." David said,

"Well, we knew at the outset that Hindus would be the dominant community. The point of this exercise was to find out if other communities were well represented."

Nathan told him, "Going by what we found, I would say that the total population of the three areas would be somewhere around twelve to fifteen thousand. That is if we take an average family size of four. So let us say a population of fourteen thousand. Out of that, I would estimate a population of around three thousand Muslims and maybe two thousand five hundred Christians with the rest being broadly labelled as Hindus." David said, "Well, we won't need to subdivide the Hindu segment, because the other two communities make up around one third of the total and that's a large segment!" He thanked Loganathan for his time and Ramya said, "I'll just drop him off and come right back. He came with us, so his bike is left at the Department."

When Ramya returned, David told her, "There are two more interviews that I've been listening to. Once you listen to them we are done for today and we'll take the next steps tomorrow." They sat down and listened to the two interviews from the footage. One was a senior journalist named Mahesh who said, "Nearly two or three years back I had written an article on the dangers of an unguarded water supply, but no one took it seriously. I had warned then that this exact thing could happen. Someone could poison our water supply and the results would be catastrophic, but at that time people told me that I was a doomsday guy and that such a thing was barely conceivable." The anchor said, "I think I remember that article. You had said that the water in our dams could be contaminated with poison. If I remember correctly, people at that time said that even if poison was dumped into the dams it would become diluted and that there were purification stations when the water left the dam."

Mahesh said, "Yes, that's what they said, and I told them that two drones could drop a very large quantity of poison into any one of our dams. I told them that the so-called purification stations did not really purify the water, it just tried to remove the silt and other floating objects. Even now I am sure that those purification stations cannot remove poison from the water! Now this has happened in a Dalit village with a small overhead tank, but what about the large overhead tanks, what about the large sumps that collect and then pump the water uphill? What if one of *those* are targeted? But I tell you that even now the authorities are not listening. Only when someone carries out a mass attack of this kind will they all sit up and pay attention!"

The second footage was about another writer named Prakash who said, “It is sad when such things happen because it just shows to what levels a human being can go down to. This will be the work of some idiot who wanted to teach the Dalits a lesson, I’m sure.” The anchor said, “Yes, most probably that will turn out to be true. But you had once written about a mass attack where the water supply was contaminated with poison and that is what I wanted to talk to you about. When you had written that story it wasn’t very well received, was it?” The writer, Prakash, smiled at her and said, “Thanks for being kind, but that story was rejected outright. No one was willing to publish it, because one publisher said that the story wasn’t quite believable and another publisher actually said that other authors had written novels about such hypothetical events and there was nothing new in it.”

The anchor asked him, “So how did you feel about it at the time and do you feel vindicated now?” The writer sighed and said, “Rejection is part and parcel of this profession and I always accept it gracefully. But in this case what irritated me was that I wasn’t just trying to sell a hypothetical story. I was worried at the lack of security where our water supply was concerned, and I had also written an article saying that the authorities should tighten things up before some fanatic actually poisoned our water! But no one listened!" The anchor asked him, "Do you think they are listening now?" Prakash shook his head and said, "I doubt it because I don't see anything being done to tighten security. They are saying that this was just an opportunistic act, that the chance was there and so some idiots did it. I'm afraid that sometimes people will only learn the hard way!" The anchor asked him, "You're saying that this could happen again?"

Prakash shrugged and replied, "It might, or something on a larger scale might happen and then I'll bet that no one will say that my story wasn't, and I quote, quite believable, or as the other guy said, hypothetical!" After listening to the footage, Ramya asked David, "So what now? What about the demographics? Are you now ruling out a terror attack?" David admonished her by saying, "I told you that anything that creates terror is a terror attack! What you mean is, am I ruling out an attack by a terrorist cell?" Ramya said, "Yes, I guess that's what I'm saying." David told her, "The agencies will anyway pursue that angle so I don't have to. But to me, the demographics are saying that this wasn't an attack by a terrorist cell."

Ramya remarked, "So, a lunatic! I'm sorry, what was it you said? Not a lunatic but..." David told her, "An insane mind. I told you there's a difference. This person will appear quite normal, he will not be stumbling along the road talking to himself, nor will he be found laughing hysterically and maybe claiming to be friends with demons! This person would have become fixated on something at some point in time and that fixation would have become an obsession and his mind would have turned insane. But only on that one point! With everything else in his daily life his mind would be quite normal."

Ramya asked him, "So he isn't really totally insane?" David said, "I would have to meet and evaluate this person to know, but eventually, without therapy, he will turn totally insane." Ramya asked him, "So what's our next move?" David told her, "As I said, I will need to meet and talk to these people face to face. I will talk to Raj and we can then go and meet these people with a cover story." She asked him, "Okay, and the cover story will be?" David thought for a bit and then replied, "We can say that we are following up with people who have voiced their concerns over the attack on the Dalit village. We just want to know if, besides the television debates and interviews, they shared their views with anyone else."Ramya said, "And then we follow whatever leads we get from those conversations. Okay, so when do we start?" David told her, "Well, you can sort them out in order of distance and we can start first thing tomorrow morning."

Before going to bed, David called his wife Rani. He told her what he was planning on doing and what he hoped to find out when he started interviewing the people that they had culled from the television footage. Rani said, "David, please be careful. I haven't forgotten about that psychopath who targeted you and the rest of us. That was a terrible time!" But David told her, "I'm sure that this person is not a true psychopath, but rather someone whose mind has gone insane. If you recall, during that time when the psychopath was targeting me, I was reviewing all my old cases to see if there was a connection. I had then told you about the case of Sarojini and I had ruled her out because I had said that she wasn't a true psychopath."

Rani said, "I think I recall something like that." David explained and said, "She was the girl who had fallen in love with Harish, but it was unrequited love. She could not believe that he did not love her and she became fixated on convincing him that he actually did love her. That fixation, over the years, became an obsession and her mind had gone insane on that one point. When you spoke to her you would not realise that she was insane, because in everything else her mind was quite sane. But when you spoke about Harish, then the change would happen and you could see that her mind had gone insane." Rani said, "Yes, I remember now. She hired men and she killed him and she planned to kill his wife as well but you caught her before she could do that." David told her, "Yes, and I believe that this case is similar. If this is not the work of a terror cell, then I think that it is the work of an insane mind."

Rani was curious now and said, "But from what I have learned from you over the years, this is how a psychopath also works. You have always said that a psychopath has no emotion and would be capable of doing exactly what has been done there now." David agreed but told her, "A psychopath will not usually commit a one-off crime. To a psychopath's mind there is always a rational explanation for what he or she does. That psychopath who came after me, both he and his brother tortured people because they believed that they were studying how much pain a human being could bear. When he came after me it was because, in his mind, it was a challenge to see who was the better man. That he had to kill and torture people for that challenge did not bother him in the least." Rani said, "So you are saying that a psychopath would not carry out a mass killing just once." David said, "Exactly! For a psychopath there has to be something that is personal. Maybe they decide to kill anyone who insults them, or they have a desire, at least in their minds, to learn something or to study something. This type of random mass killing does not have the stamp of a true psychopath. At least, that is, in my opinion." Rani sighed and said, "Your opinion is good enough for me. I always fear that someday some other psychopath may try to target you like before."

INTERVIEWS

MAY 17, MONDAY

DAVID AND RAMYA

THE FIRST PERSON David and Ramya went to see was the environmental activist named Swarna. From the footage that Ramya had culled, they had chosen only to talk to people who were local or living in the state, because as David had told her, "For someone from another state to have the knowledge of local conditions and to be able to select a target like this seems highly unlikely to me. It may be possible, but for now, I think we will concentrate on the local people." Ramya had then said, "But some of them are living quite far from here, so shouldn't we also rule them out?" But David replied, "They could very well have relatives or close friends in this area and they could be frequent visitors. We will know when we talk to them, but you could also check through social media and news accounts to see if any of them have contacts over here. Some of them are anyway living close enough to be able to carry out something like this."

Swarna was living in the next district, and David and Ramya drove there and went to her house. Ramya introduced herself as a Sub-Inspector of police and told Swarna that they were just following up with people who had stated on television that the Dalit village attack could be replicated on a larger scale. Swarna said in surprise, "But that was just a logical assumption! So what are you asking me? Did I hear it from someone, or are you thinking that I am somehow responsible for this poison attack?" David slipped in smoothly and said, "Well, yes and no! Even *I* made that assumption when the first incident happened. I mean, anyone with a sense of logic would make that assumption! And no, we don't think that you are responsible for this attack." Swarna exclaimed, "Well! I'm glad you understand! I had nothing to do with this latest attack."

Ramya asked her, "But as an environmental activist, you are concerned about the pollution of our water bodies?" She frowned and then exclaimed fiercely, "Of course I am! People just don't care about the environment. Our rivers and streams and even our underground water are being polluted on a daily basis and yet people just don't care. It will take a catastrophe for people to learn to care!" Ramya said, "Something like this latest attack on the water supply?"

Swarna started to say something but stopped and stared at her for a moment. Then she exclaimed angrily, "So you really think that I had something to do with this attack?" David said calmly, "We certainly don't think that you had anything to do with this attack. No, this is just routine, but it's something that we have to do. Let me ask you a few questions, and then we are done." Swarna said, "Well, let's not stand at the front door. Come in, please, and sit down."

When they were seated, she told David, "Nowadays people think that if you are fighting to save the environment, then you're capable of doing dangerous stuff, but that's just so not true!" David gave her a reassuring smile and said, "That's only because the term 'environmental terrorist' has spread a bit, thanks to the internet!" Then, turning serious, he asked her, "Did someone mention to you that an attack of this kind could happen? Did you read about it maybe? I'm talking now about the time before your appearance on television. Please think and try to remember if any such thing occurred." Swarna was emphatic, "Absolutely not! In fact, only when I was on the debate did the thought strike me that a psychopath could very well do something like this on a large scale using insecticide or something."

David then asked her, "Now think carefully before answering my next question. After that television appearance, did you talk about it to anyone or..." She started to reply and he said, "Let me complete, please. Did you talk about it to anyone or did anyone talk about it to you? More importantly, did anyone contact you and talk about what you had said in that debate, maybe to praise your way of thinking or to just agree with what you had said. Take your time and think about it and then tell me."

Swarna was silent for a long while, and David waited patiently. Finally, speaking slowly, she said, "I'm sure I didn't talk about it to anyone nor did anyone talk about it to me, but...I did receive a call one day..." Ramya interrupted and asked her, "Did you know the caller?" But David signalled her with his hand to stay quiet and calmly told Swarna, "You take your time and think it out." She said, "No, I didn't know the caller. I got a call and a man said that I was right in what I had predicted. I remember I asked who was calling me and he cut the call immediately. I didn't think anything about it at the time, and I still don't know if it matters. I get calls sometimes from strangers who praise me for fighting for the environment, and they don't always identify themselves."

David told her, “Of course, it happens. But if you don’t mind, would you cast your mind back to that phone call and try and tell me the exact words that this anonymous caller said?” Swarna bit her lip while she thought and then finally she said, “I’m not a hundred per cent sure, but I think he said, ‘I heard you on television and your prediction is absolutely right because our water supply system has no security. But I think you might be wrong about the insecticide.’ I’m pretty sure that’s what he said, and when I asked who he was, he cut the call.”

David had a gleam in his eye, and he asked her, “Do you remember when you got this call? The date and the time perhaps?” She shrugged and said, “It was some time ago and I get so many calls that I just don’t remember.” But David persisted and said, “Think back to that television debate and take it from there. How many days after that did you get the call?” She gave him a look of surprise and then frowned and said, “Hold on a minute and let me think.” She stared at her feet while she thought, and after a while, she said, “It was two days after the debate. I remember the next day I was watching the debate on television, and the day after that I got the call. I remember thinking at the time that at least people were watching the debate.”

David then told her, “Now think about that particular day. Start with when you got up, what you did as soon as you got up, and then go progressively forward from there until you got the call." She again gave him a look of surprise and then frowned as she thought. Finally, she said, "I think it was in the afternoon, somewhere between 3 to 5 p.m., because I had finished lunch at around 3 o'clock and I left the house at around 5 o'clock and I got the call after my lunch and before I left the house. I'm pretty sure about that!" David thanked her for her cooperation and he and Ramya left the house.

David told Ramya, "She got the date and she narrowed it down to 3 to 5 p.m., so you should be able to get her call records for that time and maybe we can trace who made that call." She asked him, "You think that call is important?" He shrugged and replied, "It might be. What I found interesting was his comment that Swarna might be wrong about the insecticide! It may mean nothing but it may mean everything." She looked confused and said, "Now you've lost me. Please explain that rather cryptic remark." David looked at her for a moment and then said, "It could just be somebody who meant that instead of insecticide an attacker could use something worse. But if it was our man, then he said that because he knew he was going to use arsenic trioxide."

Ramya's face cleared and she said, "Yes, that sounds about right. You know what I found interesting?" David told her, "That sounds like a rhetorical question." She said, "The way you got her to remember the date and then to go further and remember the time!" He shrugged and told her, "That is just a simple tool in psychology. You can think of it as an association of events and thoughts that trigger recollection. If you think back and remember what you had for breakfast, then you can take it from there. If you remember you had a sandwich, then you will associate that with what you drank that morning and that will trigger the next memory and so on. You can use it to even find something that you've misplaced at home. Just start retracing your steps from the last time you remember seeing it and usually you will find the item in one of the places that you had been that day."

She was sceptical and asked him, "Give me an example." He explained, "Let's say at 3 o'clock in the afternoon you suddenly realise that you can't find your wallet. If you remember that you had your wallet at 11 a.m. because you used your credit card and replaced it in your wallet at the time, then start from there. Work your way from there; you sat at the dining table, then maybe you went to the living room and watched some TV, so search there. Then you paid for something with your credit card again, so what was it and what did you do after that. Then lunch, and then did you lie down in your bed for a while or the couch in the living room. Go to each place as you remember your movements and I guarantee that you will find it." Ramya said, "That's fascinating! I'm going to try it as soon as I can!" David told her dryly, "Right now we have something *more* fascinating to follow up on. Let's go call on the social activist Faisal Ahmed." She smiled and replied, "Yes, of course, he lives just an hour away from here, so he's next on our list."

SWARNA

After David and Ramya had gone, Swarna sat for a long time simply staring at the wall and thinking. 'An environmental terrorist,' she thought to herself. 'It was so easy to label people nowadays. But who were the real environmental terrorists? What about the companies that knowingly polluted the rivers and streams, just so that they could make some extra profit? Weren't they the terrorists of the environment? What about the cutting down of trees to clear large tracts of forest land for the purpose of building roads or putting up more industrial units? Who were the terrorists, the ones who blew up the construction equipment or the ones who were cutting down the trees! Maybe you sometimes needed strong action to make people realise the importance of saving the environment.'

Swarna came from a poor background and she had lived in a slum area until she was nine years old. Her parents were hard workers and before she had turned ten, they had moved out of the slum to a better locality. She was their only child and they worked hard and educated her. She knew the sacrifices that her parents made and she knew how hard they worked, and in return, she excelled in her studies. She went to college on a full scholarship and majored in environmental science and technology.

She worked for five years and earned enough to make her parents comfortable and then she became an activist. She still worked and earned a very good salary, but at the same time, she was an extremely vocal environmental activist.

There was a reason why she had chosen to study environmental science. When her family had lived in the slums, there were always outbreaks of diseases. Her parents had taught her to always drink only boiled water and not to eat the savouries that were sold by the street side vendors. They had explained to her many times about water pollution and food contamination. By the time she was seven years old, she would ask her parents incessant questions on how the water became polluted, how food became contaminated, and who was responsible for the outbreak of diseases that she witnessed every year in the slum area. When she was eight years old, two of her best friends died from cholera. That was when her parents redoubled their efforts to move out of the slums, and they succeeded within two years. But Swarna never forgot the slums, and the more she learned about the environment as she grew, the more passionate she became about saving it.

INTERVIEWS

MAY 17, MONDAY

DAVID AND RAMYA

FAISAL AHMED, social activist, was a very busy man and they caught him just as he was leaving his house. They introduced themselves and he told them, “Is this urgent? I’m on my way to talk to a Dalit family who says that their child was humiliated in school by the teacher!” David told him, “I can see that you’re very passionate about fighting injustice.” Faisal’s eyes lit up as he replied fiercely, “You’re right, but not injustice in general, but the injustice that the poor and downtrodden face every day in this country of ours!” David asked him, “So the incident of the faeces in the overhead tank in the Dalit village must have affected you a lot.” Faisal’s face turned red as he exclaimed, “Can you imagine it? Can you imagine the perverted mind that even *thought* of such a despicable thing? How low can a human being sink to? I always refrain from calling such people animals, because to me that is an insult to the animals!"

David agreed and asked him, "In your interview with the television channel, you spoke about the danger of poison being used instead of faeces and a large overhead tank being selected instead of a local small one. What made you think of that?" Faisal gave him a steady look and said, "You think I'm guilty of doing that? I heard about what happened, and unfortunately it was just as I predicted. The authorities did not wake up after what happened. After all, what is a small Dalit village to them!" David said mildly, "They are still in fact investigating that incident, but I agree that they should have tightened security after that."

Faisal made a derisive sound and said, "I can guarantee you that if that had been an upper caste village instead of a Dalit one, the response would have been faster and the culprit nabbed long before this!" David still spoke calmly and asked him, "What I am interested in is simply this. Did you hear about that idea of poison and a large overhead tank being used from someone, or did you think of it yourself? Please try to recollect before answering."

Faisal started to speak but then stopped and

scratched his head. After a while, he said, "No, I'm sure no one spoke to me about it. During the interview there was some talk of something like that happening again and it just struck me that logically this could have been worse. Someone could use poison in a large tank and then a great number of people would be affected." He paused and stared at David for a moment and then said, "If you think that I had anything to do with what happened the other day, then think again. I'm a Muslim; therefore, I must be suspect won't work here because I was in Chennai for the last ten days and I just arrived home this morning. You can find enough proof of what I'm saying so please go and check!" David said placatingly, "I'm not a person who believes in such things. I'm following another angle to this case. You say that no one spoke to you about something like this happening before that interview, but did anyone talk to you or comment about what you said *after* the interview?"

Faisal frowned and looked at him and then suddenly his eyes opened wide and he exclaimed, "Of course! David Joseph! *The* David Joseph!" Ramya hid a smile and David's face had a deadpan expression as he asked him again, "So did anyone talk to you about that interview? Please think carefully and then tell me." Faisal bit his lip while he thought, but after a while he shook his head and said, "No, I'm sure no one mentioned anything to me about that interview." David asked him, "Maybe you got a phone call and someone congratulated you or agreed with what you said?" But Faisal was positive and said, "I get many phone calls and I remember every one of them. In my profession, it's a good trait to have. No, no phone call and no one spoke to me either. Is it important?"

But David just shrugged and said, "Just a routine follow-up, hoping to get some lead." Faisal said, "So the police still haven't caught the culprit. Well, maybe I'm wrong then about the Dalit village incident. Maybe a psycho like this is hard to catch!" David immediately asked him, "You think a psycho was responsible for this incident?" Faisal shrugged and said, "Stands to reason, don't you think? Who else would want to kill so many people without any reason whatsoever? Now I'm thinking that maybe a psycho is also responsible for the Dalit village incident?"

David thanked him for his time and let him go. Ramya said, "Well, what do you think? Do you think he's a possible?" David told her, "Tell me what *you* think." She thought about it and then said, "No, I don't think he fits your profile." David asked her, "And why do you think that?" She said, "He's only interested in getting justice for the downtrodden, he doesn't seem interested in revenge." She paused and then asked him, “But you also said that this insane person would appear normal except for his obsession, so how do you actually judge?” David told her, “Watch their expressions and especially their eyes. Did you notice his eyes light up and his fierce expression when he was talking about the injustice done to Dalits? That’s his focal interest in life, but I don’t think it’s an obsession. I think he just has a passion for his work.”

FAISAL

After they had left him, Faisal sat down on his front doorstep and frowned. 'Maybe they did think that he was responsible for the poisoning,' he thought. 'How active the police were now after this incident. I bet those areas are populated mainly by the upper castes and the well-to-do! A poor Dalit village is of no consequence, but when the ante is upped then they pull out all the stops.' He frowned again and thought, 'But did they really suspect him? Well, let them suspect and be damned! They were not going to find any evidence to connect him to the crime.'

Faisal Ahmed was the third son in a wealthy Muslim family. They owned a string of departmental stores, and his two brothers had joined the family business. Faisal had always been the contrary child who would question everything that was taken for granted by his two elder brothers. As a child, he had many friends, but his parents were a bit disconcerted to find that he had more friends from poor families than from his own social milieu. By the time he was in college, his parents had become resigned to the fact that he would always be asking for money to help out some friend. The only stipulation that they put on his demands was that the money had to be used for the purpose of education or health; otherwise, they would refuse.

During his college years, Faisal became involved with the more militant Muslim youth who felt that they were being denied their rights and that the Muslim community was being targeted for their religion and their way of life. When the spectre of terrorism raised its head, Faisal was angry that a Muslim had to wear his patriotism on his sleeve or be immediately labelled as a supporter of terrorism.

But the turning point in his life happened at the end of his college days. His college group had gone to a village for a project that they were working on. It was there that Faisal realised that there was a community in the country that had more to complain about than the Muslims, and that was the Dalits or Harijans. What struck him the most was that this lowest community in the caste hierarchy seemed to just accept their fate as something that could not be changed. He later learnt all about the Dalits and came to know that they could also be militant and that they sometimes had great leaders who had lifted them up and got them their rights to a certain extent.

After college, he did the bare minimum of work in the family business and devoted the rest of his time to being a social activist. He became very passionate about his work and he would use his personal money at times to file cases in court to fight and get justice for some atrocity that was committed against the Dalits. He had formed a social organisation for the help and protection of Dalits and he had persuaded his family to be the largest donor. The incident of the faeces being dumped in the overhead tank in the Dalit village had enraged him, and he had gone to the extent of filing a case against the local police for not taking action sooner than they had. The case was thrown out of court, but he still maintained that had the same incident taken place in an upper-caste village then the response would have been swift and sure!

INTERVIEWS

MAY 17, MONDAY

DAVID AND RAMYA

THEIR NEXT CALL was on Rajesh, the political analyst. He invited them in and when they were seated he asked them, "Would you like a tall cool drink? This summer the heat is really terrible!" They politely declined and David told him, "We're just following up on the television debates that dealt with the Dalit village incident. You had said that the incident could give people ideas about doing the same thing on a larger scale. Did someone suggest that to you before the debate or did you just think of it?" Rajesh frowned and said, "You're not thinking that what I said led to this recent incident?" David said, "No, no, I am just asking you if anyone had suggested something like that to you." Rajesh shook his head and said, "No, no one spoke to me about it. Besides, what I was referring to was the terrible thought that someone might contaminate a main source of water and then an outbreak like dysentery or diarrhoea or something like that could happen. I remember at the time that I thought a loony with extreme political views might do something on those lines to embarrass the government, but I never thought that someone would actually *poison* the water supply! It's obvious that there's a psycho on the loose!"

Ramya asked him, "You are a political analyst and you're not a supporter of this government, aren't you?" Rajesh gave her a patronising smile and said, "A political analyst is independent, Sub-Inspector, and just analyses politics." But Ramya told him, "Theoretically you're right, but practically, every analyst shades their analysis to support the ideology that they believe in." The patronising smile slid off his face like butter from a hot griddle and he said, "What has all that got to do with this matter?" She asked him, "Your political views are more towards the far right, aren't they? And this government is more centre-left oriented." Rajesh became a little agitated and he asked her, "What are you saying?" She shrugged and said, "You were saying in the television interview that a calamity like this could embarrass the government. I was just wondering if the wish could be the father to the thought!"

Now Rajesh was really agitated and he exclaimed, "Are you accusing me of poisoning the water tank?" Ramya shrugged again and said calmly, "I'm not accusing you of anything, I'm just asking questions. Maybe you mentioned this thought to someone and maybe that someone decided to act on it?" David was watching Rajesh closely and now he said, "We have to follow up on whatever leads we can generate. To be honest, there isn't much to go on in this case right now." There was a visible sign of relief on Rajesh's face as he said, "Well...I can understand that, I guess! But I had nothing to do with this, believe me! When I made those comments, it just seemed obvious to me that someone might think of doing something like that. But poisoning? No, this has to be the work of a psycho!"

David asked him, "So you don't think this was a terror attack?" Rajesh made a rude noise and said, "I know that's what the investigating agencies are claiming, but they're wrong. Those areas are inhabited by all castes and creeds, so who was the terrorist targeting? No, I'm sure that this was the act of a psycho and the Dalit village incident was the trigger for it." They thanked him for his time and left.

RAJESH

Rajesh was in deep thought for a long time after they had left. Did they suspect him? But that was absurd! Didn't they say that they had nothing to go on? But then again, the police always said that in the beginning of an investigation, didn't they? Of course, he had nothing to hide because he didn't do anything, but still...there was that guy, the party's district leader that he had spoken to after the interview. The guy had been quiet and thoughtful at the time...Rajesh shook his head and got up. 'No,' he thought. 'There was nothing in that. It was just that Sub-Inspector saying those things that got me worked up.'

Rajesh was born in an upper-middle-class family who believed in the far-right ideology, and he had imbibed those teachings from childhood. As he grew up and later as an adult, he fully believed in the rights of the majority over the minorities. He had joined the far-right political party but had dropped out after three years because he could not stomach some of their views and some of the fanatical talk that some members indulged in. He had become a political analyst and he still believed in the rights of the majority, but he did not want to be part of or listen to some of the fanatical utterances that took place during party meetings. However, he still had his contacts and friends within the party.

INTERVIEWS

MAY 17, MONDAY

DAVID AND RAMYA

THEY WENT to the house of Hariharan, the Dalit social activist who lived just five kilometres away from the poisoned water tank. It was a medium-sized, well-maintained house and a car was parked at the side of the building. He was at home, and he told them, "I live alone and I sprained my back yesterday, so I'm sorry that I can't offer you any refreshments. But please sit down and tell me what brings the police to my home." David told him, "It's about those television debates that dealt with the incident at the Dalit village." Hariharan frowned and said, "I know I said some politically incorrect stuff in one or two of those debates, but I meant every word of it. Whatever anyone may claim, the fact is that if a Dalit is attacked no one really cares. Oh, I know all the politically correct noises will be made, but people don't really *care*!" David said, "You feel very strongly about that, don't you?" Hariharan stared at him for a moment and then said fiercely, "I'm a social activist *and* a Dalit, so damn right I feel strongly about it!" David said mildly, "And you also feel a bit guilty."

Hariharan raised his eyebrows in surprise and stared at David. He started to say something but stopped and frowned instead. Then his face cleared and he said, "Of course, David Joseph! Well, I guess there's no point in denying it to *you*, so yes, I have always felt a bit guilty." Ramya had a confused look on her face and she said, "I'm not understanding any of this. Guilty of what?" David told her, "He has a sense of underlying guilt simply because he has managed to rise above the others in his community and he has tasted success. It's silly of course, because his success is largely due to his hard work and his intelligence. But there it is, that's the psychology of a good man who rises above his community."

Hariharan sighed and said, "I was in England for five years and I did well, but I had to come back and try to do something for my community. So I became a social activist and I try my best to see that my people get the education and justice that they deserve." David told him, "And that incident of the faeces in the tank really enraged you!" Hariharan said fiercely, "In our state the government really does try to uplift the backward communities, I'll give them that. But when something like this incident happens, it just shows that there are still so many people in our society who believe in the caste system and they are never going to change!" David said, "Change is always slow, but as long as there are people who want it and are willing to fight for it, then it will happen. It's just a matter of time!" Hariharan was thoughtful when he said, "I guess you're right, we did get the police reforms that no political party wanted, and that was because people were willing to fight and sacrifice for it. But for the Dalits..."

Changing the subject, David told him, "We are really here because of a suggestion you had made on one of the debates, about the possibility of a terrorist contaminating the water supply." Hariharan gave him a wry smile and said, "You are not going to accuse me of what happened the other day, are you? What, revenge for my people?" Ramya intervened and said, "You were extremely agitated in those interviews and it's obvious that what was done at that Dalit village had enraged you. So it is pretty normal for an enraged person to think of revenge."

Hariharan was immediately angry and he said, "So you *are* accusing me!" But Ramya said calmly,

"I'm not accusing you, I'm just pointing out a fact of life. Maybe you had nothing to do with this, but then again maybe you spoke to someone about your idea and that someone might have thought that it was time to take action." Hariharan jumped up and glared at her, but Ramya just regarded him calmly. Suddenly he shook his head and sat down again. "I've really got to do something about my short temper," he said with a small laugh. "So you think that I had something to do with this. Well, you can *think* that, but you are still going to have to prove it."

David spoke calmly and said, "We are not accusing you of anything. I only want to know if someone had spoken to you before that debate and made that suggestion of contaminating a larger source of the water supply. Think about it before you answer, please." Hariharan said, "I don't have to think about it because no one spoke to me about it. During the debate, the thought just occurred to me that a terrorist may very well do the same thing. You think that my suggestion may have given a terrorist the idea?"

David shrugged and then asked him, "I want you to think carefully about this next question. After the debate, did anyone talk to you about it or maybe you got a phone call?" Hariharan frowned while he thought, but then he said, "The Sub-Inspector just suggested that maybe I had spoken to someone about it and I immediately flew off the handle! But I guess what she said is logical. Now that I think of it, no one spoke to me nor did I speak to anyone about it, but I did get a phone call two days later. The guy said that I was very logical and that a terrorist could easily do the same thing." David sat up straight and there was a gleam in his eye as he told Hariharan, "I want you to think back carefully to that phone call. You are sure about the day?" Hariharan nodded and David asked him, "What about the time, do you remember when the call came in?"

Hariharan squeezed his hands together as he thought and then he said, "It would have been around 2 p.m. because I remember I had just finished my lunch." David smiled with satisfaction and then, turning serious again, he told him, "Now that your mind is at the time of the phone call, I want you to think and tell me exactly what the caller said. Don't summarise, but try to think of his exact words."

Hariharan continued to squeeze his hands together while he thought. Then he said, "He told me, 'I agree with what you said in that debate. You're right, the same thing can happen on a larger scale but the authorities are just too dumb to listen when they are told.' Then I said something that maybe the authorities would now wake up and he said, 'I doubt it, because they are not tightening their security. But I think that you are wrong about the terrorist part.' Then before I could say anything else he cut the call." David stood up and said, "Thank you, I think we're done here!" Hariharan looked at him curiously and then asked him, "You think that guy did it? You think he dumped the poison? But then he must be a psycho!" David just said, "We're working on it. Thanks again for your time."

They left and Ramya asked David, "You know that guy?" David smiled at her and said, "No, but I always do my homework! His parents and his sister were killed in a mob attack when he was a teenager, something about a love affair between his sister and a boy from an upper-caste community. It's an old story that just keeps repeating itself and it's disgusting! Anyway, he got a large government compensation and he completed his education and excelled in his studies. He then went to London on a full scholarship and he's done well in life. He's very intelligent but he came back to work as a social activist, so he has to have an underlying guilt about his success."

Ramya said, "When we watched the footage you said that he had wild-looking eyes." David told her, "And so he does, didn't you notice it? But that only happens when he's angry and not for anything in particular. He just has a pretty short temper!" Ramya remarked, "The way he jumped up, I was wondering about that sprained back." David smiled at her and said, "You don't miss much, do you! But I saw him wince as he sat down again, so I would put it down to his anger. He really needs counselling about anger management!" Ramya asked him, "So the phone call, kind of the same thing that happened with Swarna. You think the caller is the perpetrator?" He looked at her and said, "You have the timing of this call as well, so I think that you need to get the phone records for both calls on a priority basis." Ramya said, "Yes, I'll do that, but it will take two to three days."

HARIHARAN

Hariharan got up with some difficulty and went and lay down on his bed. He really would have to learn to control his temper, he thought. Did they suspect him of poisoning that water? She had spoken of revenge and he admitted to himself that he had thought of revenge for that Dalit village atrocity. But then, who wouldn't want revenge for such a dastardly deed? Besides, he was really no stranger to thoughts of revenge! The problem with the Dalits, he thought, was that they never really planned on revenge. They had been beaten down and subdued for so many centuries that it was difficult for them to throw off the yoke and rebel. But there had been Dalit leaders in the past who were strong and had led them for a short while, and then the Dalits had shown what they were capable of. What they needed right now was a strong leader who would act and could galvanise them, and then they would fight for their rights and their dignity. Yes, he thought, a strong leader...

His childhood had been a happy one and he had never really come across any caste discrimination. His parents both had government jobs under the scheduled caste quota and they were in the middle-income category. Everything was good until his sister, who was three years older than him, fell in love with an upper-caste boy in college. He loved her in return, but his parents were against it and they threatened the family. But the boy stood firm and promised to marry Hariharan's sister. Hariharan was fifteen years old when the mob came in the night and attacked his family. They beat them up and set fire to their house. His parents and his sister succumbed to their injuries and only he survived. The boy who loved his sister later committed suicide.

The case dragged on and on and finally a few people were convicted and given life imprisonment. Hariharan got a huge compensation from the government and he used it to complete his studies. He vowed at the time to get revenge for what was done to his family, but he was really good at his studies and that occupied his time and kept his mind sane. And then came the full scholarship to a college in England and thoughts of revenge took a backseat. He excelled in college as well and later worked in England for about five years. But the thoughts of what had happened to his family and what was still happening to his community finally took him back to India where he became a Dalit activist. He had majored in humanities and social sciences and he still gave lectures in England and in colleges in the country. He also did online tutoring for students in

India and in England as well. Now he was independently wealthy and he devoted most of his time to his social activities for the Dalit community. But the trauma of that fifteen-year-old boy had never really left him!

INTERVIEWS

MAY 17, MONDAY

DAVID AND RAMYA

THEY MET the senior journalist Mahesh at a restaurant after talking to him on the phone when they found that he wasn't at home. David told him, "I have only two questions for you. The suggestion you made on the TV debates, was that only because of your article or did someone also speak to you about it before the debate?" Mahesh said, "Everyone knows that I wrote that article about two or three years ago, although no one listened at the time. But no one spoke to me about it before the debate." David asked him, "And after the debate? Did you get any phone call or did someone talk to you about it?" Mahesh gave him a curious look and said, "It's funny you should ask me that. After the debate, my friends and family all spoke to me about it. They said that I was vindicated after all these years, that now no one would call me a doomsday prophet...you know, things like that. But I did get a phone call and..."

But David cut him off and said, "Please wait! I want you to think carefully before you get to that phone call." He made a movement of his hand from left to right before Mahesh's face and said, "I want you to go back in your mind to that debate and remember things from there until you get to the phone call." Mahesh said very seriously in a monotone, "These are not the droids you are looking for." For a second they stared at each other and then they both laughed. Mahesh said, "Sorry, I just couldn't resist...the way you moved your hand in front of my face..." Ramya was perplexed and asked, "What was that about...droids??" Mahesh gave her a rueful smile and said, "Before your time, Sub-Inspector. *Star Wars*, the movie."

Turning serious, he told David, "I don't have to think about it because I remember the date. It was two days after the debate and it would have been around 3 p.m., no doubt about it." David asked him, "What made it stick in your mind?" Mahesh shrugged and replied, "I'm a journalist and anything odd sticks in my mind, and this phone call *was* odd!" David said, "Tell me the exact words that were spoken if you can recall." Mahesh said, "Oh yes I can! He said, 'You were right three years ago and you are right even now. No one is listening, but they will listen soon, believe me.' And then he cut the call." He gave David a look of surprise and said, "You think that...I should have thought of it myself, but repeating it just now brought it all back and connected it. The poisoning of the water sump?"

David nodded and told him, "That's what I think but I have a way to go before I get to the answer. You've been a great help because I was starting to doubt myself!" As they started to leave, Ramya told Mahesh, "I've also seen *Star Wars* by the way. I just didn't connect it in the moment!" Mahesh told her ruefully, "You and me both. I should have connected that phone call!" As they left, David's phone rang and he spoke briefly. When they were outside the restaurant he told Ramya, "That was Raj. He wants to see me right now, so I guess we'll have to go back to the station. How many more people are left for me to see?" Ramya said, "Just two, both are writers." David said, "Okay, we'll get to them after we talk to Raj." He looked at the time and then said, "But it's already 5.15 in the evening, so we may have to see those two only tomorrow morning."

INVESTIGATIONS

MAY 17, MONDAY

THE POLICE

WHILE DAVID WAS INTERVIEWING the people connected to the television debates, the police and the central investigating agencies were questioning and rounding up suspected members of terrorist cells. These were people who had some connection with convicted or accused bomb blast perpetrators. Some of the convicted men had connections to the Islamic State or ISIS, while others were suspected of being part of or had received aid from terror outfits like the Lashkar-e-Taiba and others. The central agencies were talking to the men in prison and checking if there had been any chatter among the terror outfits about a possible mass poisoning plan. Locally, the central agencies, with the cooperation of the state police, were questioning and checking on the movements of the local suspects.

Inspector Jamal of the national investigating agency was at the house of one of the suspects. He was accompanied by Superintendent of Police Raj Kumar of the state crime branch and they were talking to the mother of a young man, Kaleem, who was suspected of having links with some of the men who had been arrested the previous year. The mother, Fatima, was saying that her son was not at home. Inspector Jamal said, "I'm sure that you can tell me where your son is, Madam. We just need to question him regarding his movements on a certain day this month." Fatima said, "You mean you are looking for a chance to arrest him! Being a Muslim has now become a curse in this country!" Inspector Jamal said mildly, "I think you know that it is only a curse for the youth who believe in the preaching of fanatics and resort to criminal acts."

Fatima said fiercely, "If something happens, then the first house that the police visit will be a Muslim home. We are suspect just by being Muslim!" Raj told her, "Mother, you know that is not true. After the new police reforms were carried out, we work independently and not under political pressure. Your son has proven connections with men who carried out bomb blasts and the police found literature of some Islamic terror outfits on his laptop. Therefore, he is under surveillance, and the fact of him being a Muslim has nothing to do with it."

Fatima suddenly broke down and began crying. Through her sobs she said, "I had warned him so many times not to move around with those people, but he claimed that they were just good friends of his. Even what was found on his laptop was what one of those friends had sent him. His father is dead and he doesn't have a dominant male member in the family to look up to, so he is easily persuaded to believe anything by these so-called friends."

Inspector Jamal told her, "Your son is not alone in this. There are many youths in this country who are being misguided by the fanatics. SP Raj Kumar tells me that the local police have set up a unit called the 'brothers and sons of the police' and they hold regular meetings and do their best to counter the influence of these fanatics. You should get your son to join them." She sighed and said, "I didn't know that. I will talk to him about it and I'll get him to join them. He has realised his mistake in believing those people and now he has nothing to do with any of them. He's a good boy and he now works hard to provide for his sisters." Raj gave her his card and told her, "Ask him to call me and I will see that he joins our group. You must have heard about the poisoning of the water tank in New Town. That is why we are questioning all those with links to terror outfits, and your son is known to be a sympathiser."

Suddenly a young man walked into the house and asked Fatima, "Mother, what do they want?" Inspector Jamal turned to him and answered, "We just want to ask you a few questions and then we will leave." The young man went and sat down and gave Inspector Jamal a defiant look. "I'm not afraid of you anymore. I have done nothing wrong in the past and I will do nothing wrong in the future. So hounding me will get you nothing, unless of course you want to produce fake evidence and arrest me!" Inspector Jamal said calmly, "You were under surveillance only because those men who carried out the bomb blasts were your friends and the police found terrorist literature on your laptop. They did not arrest you but just kept you under surveillance. So how was that not fair?"

Kaleem cast his eyes down and muttered, "I'm smarter now and I am careful in choosing my friends." Jamal said, "That's good and I'm proud of you if you have realised the folly of trusting false prophets. But we are not here for what happened in the past. You must have heard about the poisoning of the water in New Town and we are trying to find out if there has been any talk or rumours about such a thing being planned." Kaleem looked up at him and said, "I don't keep in touch with any of my former friends, but I can tell you that if such talk or rumours were doing the rounds, then most youngsters would eventually have heard about it. But there has been nothing." Raj told him about the group that the police had formed. He told him, "I gave my card to your mother and I hope that you will call me. We have started this group specifically for youngsters like you. You will meet others who have had similar experiences and it will help you. You won't have to be alone any longer."

They left the house and Raj told Jamal, "I believe that boy when he says that there has been no chatter about a possible poisoning attack. I think he has genuinely reformed and he doesn't believe his former friends anymore. Your people have picked up many such youngsters and you are also questioning those in prison. Have you made any progress as yet?" Jamal replied, "It will take time, but we will get there." Raj was doubtful and said, "I'm beginning to wonder if David was right and this is not the work of a terror cell."

Inspector Jamal stopped short and looked at him. "What is it you're saying?" he asked him. Raj shrugged and said, "David looked into the demographics of those three areas, and given the results of what he found he believes that this is the act of a lone person, a psycho." Jamal asked him in a harsh tone, "Why weren't we told of this? I thought that the local police were cooperating with us on this investigation!" Raj gave him a look of surprise and said, "We *are* cooperating! David is an independent person and he has helped us in solving many a difficult case in the past. He is in no way interfering with your investigation, so what are you getting worked up about?" Jamal was immediately contrite and he said, "I'm sorry, I didn't mean it to sound like that. It's only that we all know who David Joseph is, and if he has another take on this attack, then I for one definitely want to know about it. Can we go right now and talk to him?"

MAY 17, MONDAY - EVENING

INSPECTOR JAMAL

DAVID AND RAMYA walked into Raj's office at the city police headquarters and Raj introduced David to Inspector Jamal. Raj then told David, "I mentioned to the Inspector about your take on this poison attack and he feels that we should have consulted with him." Inspector Jamal immediately said, "I did not quite say that! I said that we should have been told that you had another idea about this attack." David said mildly, "And if Raj had told you and you had abandoned your line of investigation and pursued mine and it turned out that I was wrong, then what?" Jamal said, "Well we won't abandon our line of investigation, but we can also pursue your idea and see what we come up with."

David sighed and said, "And that is precisely why I did not want to tell you. This type of investigation has to be conducted discreetly, whereas, if you will forgive me, your people would tackle it like a bull in a china shop!"

Jamal smiled and said, "We are not that bad! I believe that nowadays we have improved a lot." But David said, "If my theory is true and this is in fact the work of an insane mind, then the police barging in and questioning everyone would alert the perpetrator." Jamal shrugged and said, "So what, he would try to run away? He would try to hide evidence? If he runs we can find him and running away would be an admission of guilt." David said grimly, "If he is alerted, I am not worried about him trying to run away. I am worried that he would carry out another attack!"

Raj, Jamal, and Ramya together exclaimed, "What?!!" Raj said, "David you can't be serious! If you are right and this is an insane person, why would he try to carry out another attack? Besides, if he does try then he will fail because all water supply routes are now guarded." Jamal said, "Well, if he is insane, then knowing that security has been tightened may not deter him. But that will only help us to catch him if he dares to try it again."

David told Raj, "There are actually three questions in what you have asked me. Am I serious? Of course I am! You said if this is an insane person then why would he carry out another attack? I've told you this before but I'll tell you again..." But he was cut off by Ramya who said, "He is not an insane person per se. He has an insane mind!" Jamal looked at her and then looked at David, "That sounds like psychology to me, but this is a crime and we'll get the criminal, insane or not. All I am asking is that you share your findings with us and we'll pursue that as well." He added, "In the interests of justice." David regarded him for a moment and then said, "We have been listening and watching the footage of television debates and interviews with regard to the Dalit village incident. We have specifically narrowed it down to people who spoke about the concept of the same thing being carried out on a larger scale, and we are talking to them."

Jamal asked him, "You think they may be involved? You think that they may have mentioned the same thing to someone else and..." He stopped and thought for a while and then said, "Yes, I can see that. Someone may have got the idea from one of those debates or interviews, but it still doesn't rule out the terrorist angle. A terror outfit may have got the idea from the debates and then carried it out." The others remained silent and did not comment and after a while Jamal said, "But talking to these people won't help in tracking down the terror cell, unless you're right and one of them is actually insane enough to carry out the attack." The others were still silent and finally Jamal asked David, "So will you share your findings with us? And what was that about the demographics of these three areas? Could you explain that to me?"

David told him, "The demographics show that there is a substantial population of all castes and creeds in the three areas, with Hindus of course being the largest. It seems to me that when a terrorist attacks he tries to send a message, but what message will he send when everyone is a victim?" Jamal shrugged and said, "It wouldn't matter to many of them if their own community people were also victims. I am saying this for all forms of terror, whether Hindu, Muslim, Christian, or caste, it doesn't matter to many of them. All they want to do is to create terror! You talk about insane? I have interrogated so many of these people and they are so indoctrinated in their beliefs that they will do anything. To me they are totally insane!" David agreed but said, "While that is true, targeting these three areas still doesn't make sense. If those groups you are talking about decided to try out this method of attack they wouldn't have chosen these three areas."

Jamal asked him, "Why do you say that?" David said, "This could only be done with local knowledge and the police do not believe that such terror outfits as you have just described exist here. They are still following the terror angle, but they are looking for a local cell that may have latched onto this idea after the Dalit village incident. So that's why I say, for a local, the demographics would matter." Jamal again asked him, "So will you share your findings with me?" David shrugged and said, "Ramya will give you everything that we have got, the demographics results and the footage of the television debates." He turned to Ramya and told her, "Give the Inspector the details from your laptop and then go home and rest. It's been a long day, so let's meet tomorrow morning."

That night when David phoned Rani he told her all that had happened during the day. When Rani had come with her daughters to stay with David at the time when the psychopath was targeting him, they had grown closer and they had talked a lot at night. Rani had expressed an interest in his cases and had asked him if he wouldn't mind talking to her about his progress in catching the psychopath. David was happy that she had taken such an interest in his work and from then it had become a habit for him to keep her informed when he was working a case.

Now Rani told him, "This young policewoman, Ramya, you are very interested in her I can tell. Hari told Devika that you seemed to be taking her under your wing." David told her what Priya had said about Ramya reminding him of Revathi. "I realised that she was right," he told her. "She does remind me of Revathi. She's tough and she's very intelligent. She seems to have a natural talent for understanding psychology as well." Rani said, "Well, I'm happy because it's been a long time since you've taken on a protégé. A man like you is born to teach and pass on your knowledge and you're actually happiest when you have a protégé." David told her that he was going to try and convince Ramya to go back to college and study psychology. Rani laughed and told him, "So she will also be a psychologist cum detective and your protégé!" They talked some more and then said their goodnights. David then spent an hour going over his notes on the case so far before going to bed.

The next morning the police picked up Faisal and Hariharan for questioning and it made the breaking news on television channels.

MAY 18, TUESDAY - MORNING

THE MAN

WHEN THE NEWS broke that Faisal and Hariharan had been picked up for questioning, the man was having his breakfast while watching the television. He had been closely following the news since May 14 and had been somewhat amused to see that the police were running in circles. He knew that the authorities had finally tightened security around the water supply routes, and he had been debating with himself whether or not he should carry out the second attack as planned. He had told himself that if the authorities had finally woken up to the danger, then he should be satisfied, and there was no need for the second attack. The whole point of what he had done was to prove to the authorities that the danger existed. He wanted them to take things seriously and not make stupid comments like doomsday prophet, hypothetical, not really believable, and more stupid things like that.

'Well,' he thought, 'they believed it now, but were they really aware of the danger, or was the present security over the water routes just a kneejerk reaction which would not last?' He had not seen anything on the news to indicate that the authorities were tightening security across other avenues of attack. Therefore, he was in two minds whether to carry out the second attack or not.

He was furious now as he watched a police spokesperson tell the media, "We are just questioning these two gentlemen to see if they have spoken to others about what they said on television. We are hoping to get a lead from them and then we will be closer to nabbing the culprit." *He thought to himself, 'They will never learn..So now they think that whoever spoke of such a possibility could be guilty? That was worse than calling them doomsday prophets and disbelieving their intellect. Now they had decided to shoot the messenger!'* He flung the plate he was holding against the wall and his mouth opened wide in a long silent scream. He pulled at his hair and his eyes turned red with a mad gleam. He pressed the palms of his hands against the sides of his head and staggered to his bathroom. Bending over the washbasin, he splashed cold water on his face. He rubbed his temples and pressed his fingers against his eyes. After some time, he straightened up and dabbed his face with a towel. His face looked normal now and his eyes no longer had that mad gleam. He calmly combed his hair as he stared at himself in the mirror. He had made up his mind!

An hour later, he went to check the equipment that he had so carefully acquired and which he was confident could not be traced back to him. At the back of his house was a shed where all the junk that he had not thrown away was stored. There was a large drum that contained a lot of odds and ends like small packets of leftover bolts and nuts, packets of nails, electrical fittings, electric wires, etc. Piled up at the back of the shed behind the drum were two ceiling fans that he had intended to get repaired but had never quite got around to. There was a pedestal fan standing in a corner, there were old car tyres and tubes, long pieces and short pieces of left-over plumbing and electrical pipes, and some old sacks and lengths of tubing and ropes. Covering most of the junk was a large tarpaulin sheet.

He pulled off the tarpaulin and carefully moved the two ceiling fans and some tyres and tubes to the side. Hidden behind them was a fogging machine that could be carried by hand and some large cans. He took them out of their hiding place and began his preparations. He was busy for more than three hours as he had to continually read a booklet that contained the instructions he needed. Although he had already done all this once and had carried out a trial run, he was still careful as he knew that a mistake could result in his death, and he wasn't ready to die yet. He was just about to complete his work when he heard the front doorbell ring and he cursed. He put everything back into the shed and, grabbing the tarpaulin, he carefully draped it over the fogger and the cans so that everything was completely covered. He stood back and looked at it and then took three old tyres and placed them over the tarpaulin. Finally satisfied, he raced back into his house.

INTERVIEWS

MAY 18, TUESDAY - MORNING

DAVID AND RAMYA

WHEN RAMYA CAME to Raj's house to meet David, she found him pacing up and down in front of the house. He stopped pacing when she got out of the car and he asked her, "Have you seen the breaking news on television?" She nodded and said, "The central agencies have moved fast it seems. But why did they only pick up Faisal and Hariharan? Do they suspect them to be involved, or have they dug up some evidence?" David shrugged and told her, "If they don't get anything useful from them, then I'm sure they will pick up the others as well." Ramya again asked him, "But why start with Faisal and Hariharan unless they have some other pieces of evidence?" David said grimly, "That is classic police thinking! Faisal is a Muslim and a social activist for Dalits. Hariharan is a Dalit *and* a social activist for Dalits!"

Ramya frowned and then said, "So they are thinking that this may have been a revenge attack for what happened in the Dalit village?" David shook his head and said irritably, "I don't know what they are thinking, and I don't care! All I'm worried about is that now a second attack may be imminent. I warned Jamal and he did not listen, so now this may trigger the second attack." Ramya said, "Yes, you said that you were worried about a second attack, but you didn't explain it at the time."

David stared at her for a moment and his face was blank. Then his face cleared and he said, "You're right, I don't think I explained it." He thought for a moment and then he told her, "All along I have been saying that this could be the work of an insane mind. Not an insane person, mind you, but an insane mind! A person who has become so fixated on one single thing that it has become an obsession with him and his mind has become insane on that one thing." Ramya sighed and told him, "I guess I'm not so smart after all because all that just went right over my head!" David gave her a fierce look for a moment and then he laughed. "Come on," he said. "Get in the car and let's go and I'll explain later." Ramya asked him, "There are two people left for you to see, Siva and Prakash. Both are writers and both have written about this kind of attack, so who do you want to see first?" David was getting into the car and he said shortly, "The nearest one." Ramya started the car and told him, "Well then, that would be Siva."

Siva lived in a large two-storied building and when they rang the front doorbell, the door was opened by a middle-aged lady who looked at them, and seeing Ramya's uniform, she exclaimed, "Hello! Is something wrong?" Ramya said, "No mother, we just want to talk to Siva. He lives here, doesn't he?" The woman stared at her suspiciously and then said in an agitated tone, "He's my son, why do you want to talk to him? He's a good boy and I'm sure he hasn't done anything wrong, so why would the police want to talk to him?" Ramya spoke calmly and told her, "I'm sure he's done nothing wrong, mother! We just want to talk to him because we think he can help us out in our investigation." The woman appeared to calm down at Ramya's tone and she said, "His father and I live down here. He lives on top because he needs peace and quiet. He's a writer, you know!" The last was said with pride and Ramya told her, "Yes mother, we know he's a writer. We'll go up and talk to him now. Sorry for disturbing you."

They walked up the outside stairs and found themselves in a long open sit-out. They went to the front door and rang the bell. After about a minute David said, “He’ll be on the phone talking to his mother.” Ramya gave him a curious look and he shrugged and remarked, “She seems the protective type.” They waited, and about five minutes later the door was opened by a lean fair man in his thirties with slightly long hair. “Come in,” he said. “What can I do to help the police?” He didn’t wait for an answer but led the way into a sitting room where he asked them to be seated. He also sat down in a straight-backed chair facing them and he again asked, “So what can I do to help the police?” David told him, “We’re just following up with everyone who did those television debates and interviews after the incident at the Dalit village.” Siva nodded his head sagely and said, “I knew that was just a precursor to the real attack. I think I said as much in that interview, but of course no one listened!”

Before David could say anything, he went on, “I even wrote a book on just such a thing happening, you know. And what was the reaction? Everyone thought it was a bit farfetched. They said that terrorists don’t carry out such blind attacks, that it wasn’t possible to poison the water in a dam as it would just get diluted and so on and so forth.” David again started to say something, but Siva wasn’t finished! “Do I feel vindicated?” he asked and then answered his own question. “Of course I do!

But what a price to pay to be proved right! Terrorists don't carry out such blind attacks! Hah!"

He was silent for a moment and seeing that he had finally run out of steam, David said, "But the police are not thinking that this is a terrorist attack." Siva almost jumped out of his chair. "What?!!" he exclaimed. "Are they mad? What more proof do they need! They are still wearing their official blinkers, damn them!" David said mildly, "They're actually thinking that this may be the work of a lone man, a mad man to be precise." Siva had sat down and now he again jumped up. "Mad?" he almost shouted. "*They* are mad, I tell you. No one really listens until it is too late. They did not listen before and they are not listening now! Mad indeed!" He took a deep breath and sat down. "Forgive me," he said. "I tend to get worked up about such stupidity. A mad man! How could a mad man have the brains to carry out such a thing? I tell you, this is the work of a terrorist and the police have to wake up and remove their damn blinkers."

David changed the subject and asked him, "At the television interview you had said all these things. What I want to ask you is if someone spoke to you about this before the interview?" Siva stared at him as though he was mad and asked him, "Why would someone talk to me about something that I have written? Didn't you hear me? I wrote a book about this and no one listened!" David said mildly, "Of course, of course. But tell me, did anyone talk to you *after* the interview? You know, to congratulate you or maybe comment on your interview or your book for that matter." Siva gave him an angry look but then suddenly looked thoughtful. David waited patiently until finally Siva said, "No one actually spoke to me about the interview or my book, but I did get a phone call. Now that I think about it, I guess it was a bit strange!"

David pounced on that word and asked him, "Strange? Tell me about it please." Siva was still thinking and he gave David a blank look and said, "Tell you about..." Then his face cleared and he said, "Oh, you mean the phone call! Yes, I got this call about two days after the interview I think...or was it three days?" He frowned and thought but then said, "Anyway, that doesn't matter. This guy said that I was right and he said that I was very clever!" David asked him, "Please concentrate on the phone call. Go back to the interview and start from there. What you did the next day, and then go from there until you received the phone call. Try and recall, please, as it is important to know the exact day that you received the call."

Siva gave him a look that clearly said that he thought David was mad. "Important?" he said. "Why would a phone call be important!" Ramya suddenly stood up and said in a stern voice, "Sir! You can either cooperate with us here and be helpful, or we can take you down to the police station and interrogate you! Make up your mind and make it up fast because this is serious and we don't have any time to waste!" As she spoke, David noticed a change in Siva's demeanour. So far he had been aggressive and self-absorbed, but as Ramya spoke his face cleared and he appeared docile and sat back limply in his chair. "Yes, yes," he said. "Of course I will cooperate. No need to shout at me, you know. You have already delayed my lunch as it is, and mother does not like me to eat out of time!"

He looked at David and asked him, "What was that you were saying?" David said, "The day of the phone call is important, so go back to the day of the interview and try to remember things from there. For example, what did you do the next day; you got up in the morning and..." He sat quietly while Siva thought. Then suddenly Siva said, "It was two days after the interview and the call came in around 2 p.m.!" David asked him, "Are you sure about the time?" Siva nodded and said, "Oh yes! Mother had called to tell me not to eat lunch so late and this call came in just after that." He paused for a moment and then added, "I was absorbed in my work that day and completely lost track of time and she was very angry. She's always been very concerned about me, you know."

David asked him, "When you wrote that book, were you disappointed at the reactions that you got?" Siva gave him a blank stare for a moment, but then he shook his head as though to bring his mind back to the present and he said, "Disappointed? Well, of course I was! Mother was very angry at some of the comments on social media. It was a well thought out book and in the story the protagonist dumps poison into the waters of the dam. People said that it wasn't feasible, that the amount of water in the dam would just dilute the poison and things like that." He paused for a moment and then exclaimed, "They missed the point of the whole story! Hah! Now that it has happened, I bet they must be feeling pretty stupid about their comments. They'll eat their words now, that's what mother says!"

David asked him, "Can you now think back to the phone call and try to tell me the exact words that the caller said?" Siva frowned and said a bit heatedly, "Of course I can! He didn't try to belittle my writing, in fact he praised me! Mother said..." But this time David interrupted him and said sternly, "The phone call! The exact words that the caller said!" Siva immediately became calmer and he said, "He told me, 'You are brilliant! Soon the authorities will realise just how right you were when you wrote that book. And the ending was just genius. Who knows, even *that* may come true!'" David's eyes had that gleam again as he asked him, "Tell me about the ending of the book!" Siva told him, "The book ends with the protagonist planning another attack but this time from the air, using drones!"

David sighed and stood up. "Thank you for your time," he said. He signalled to Ramya and they left the house. When they were outside David told her, "I want to see if there is a back staircase to the upper floor." They walked around the house and at the back they saw what looked like a fire escape ladder that reached to a door at the back of the upper floor. There was also a back entrance with a gate that led to the street. David also noticed a shed at the back of the house that seemed to contain a lot of junk, a drum, old tyres, and things like that. Ramya was curious and asked him, "Why the interest in a back entrance?" David told her, "He might have been on the phone to his mother, but he might also have just come up through the back entrance which would also account for the delay in opening the front door. A back entrance would mean that he can come and go without his mother knowing!"

When they were in the car and on their way, Ramya said, "That guy seems like a nutcase. He could fit your profile because he seems obsessed with his book and he's angry at the negative reactions to it that he got!" But David was rubbing his chin and was deep in thought and he didn't answer her. Ramya said, "David? Did you hear what I said?" David blinked and looked at her. "We still have one more guy to see," was all he said before sinking into deep thought again.

SIVA

Siva was pacing up and down in his sitting room muttering to himself when his phone rang. He picked it up and his mother said, "What did the police want with you? What did they ask you? I hope you didn't say anything stupid to give them wrong ideas!" Siva said angrily, "Mother, stop going on and on! I know how to talk and I certainly don't need you to tell me how to talk. The police wanted to know my opinion on this attack because of my book. You know the poisoning of the water in the overhead tank, they just wanted my opinion!" His mother raised her voice and said, "Oh! So you are a great man now, is it? People are now talking about your book? Just remember who gave you the idea for the book! And don't you dare to talk to me in that tone of voice! So you don't need me to tell you anything, is it? Have you had your lunch? You cannot even eat at the proper times without me reminding you. I shudder to think what will happen to you when I am dead and gone." Siva said docilely, "Yes mother, thank you, I will eat my lunch now." His mother said, "Don't just stand there talking, go and eat your lunch right now!"

Siva put down the phone and stood there for a moment with a blank look on his face. Then slowly his face changed and a look of cunning suffused his features. Aloud he said, "So you think that you can still control me, old woman! Well, let's wait and see who will have the last laugh. You think that I cannot do anything on my own, but I'll prove you wrong!" He stood there and stared at the wall. Yes, he thought to himself. I am finally going to prove her wrong once and for all and then I will be free. Free to do whatever I want without her breathing down my neck. Suddenly the cunning look left his face and he shook his head as though he was bringing himself back to the present. Aloud he said, "What am I doing just standing here. Mother told me to eat my lunch and she is going to get angry again if I don't listen to her." He quickly went and served his lunch and sat down at the table and started to eat.

Siva was the only child of Saravanan and Padmini. Saravanan was a quiet unassuming man who wanted peace in the home at any cost. Padmini was a domineering lady who ruled the house, her husband, and her son. From the time of his birth to the present, she had planned and controlled every aspect of his life leaving him no room to make his own decisions. If things worked well she took the credit and always emphasised how important she was in his life. If things went south then she scolded and blamed him for not trying hard enough. Over the years, Siva grew up believing that his mother was always right and that he would not survive without her. His father being a docile man did not help in any way in changing that belief.

But Siva was born with a bit of a stubborn streak, and although he had been suppressed by his mother for so many years, that streak was still there just waiting for a chance to break through. Over the past few years, he had slowly developed a fixation that he needed to be free of his mother. That fixation had gradually turned into an obsession and now a part of his mind was continually conjuring up plans that would give him his freedom. Those plans of late had also included the thought of murdering his mother as a final act of defiance against her authoritarianism!

INVESTIGATIONS

MAY 18, TUESDAY - MORNING

THE POLICE

THE CENTRAL INVESTIGATING agency sent two teams very early on Tuesday morning to pick up Faisal and Hariharan for questioning. When Faisal opened his front door, dressed only in a lungi and a singlet, the Inspector who was leading the team told him, “You will need to come with us immediately to the police station.” Faisal was unperturbed and asked the Inspector, “May I ask why? Am I being accused of something?” The Inspector said stolidly, “That I cannot answer. I was told to bring you in immediately for questioning and that’s all I know. You will please put on some clothes immediately and come with us.” Faisal was still unperturbed and he asked the Inspector, "And if I refuse to come with you without a proper explanation?" The Inspector promptly replied, "Then I'm afraid that I will have to arrest you!"

Faisal shrugged and said, "That's what I thought! Then I guess I had better get dressed, right? By the way Inspector, just out of curiosity, have you heard of the term Gestapo?" He turned to go inside and then asked the Inspector, "You want to accompany me while I get dressed?" The Inspector hesitated but then said, "No sir, we will wait for you here." Faisal smiled at him and said, "So you *do* know the term Gestapo. I'll just take a few minutes to throw on some clothes." He returned within five minutes and they took him to the police station where Inspector Jamal was waiting.

The second team rang the doorbell of Hariharan's home and he opened the door. The Sub-Inspector who was leading the team told him, "You are to accompany us to the police station immediately!" Hariharan stared at him for a moment and then said, "At 6 o'clock in the morning? Are you here to arrest me? And if you are then aren't you supposed to tell me why I am being arrested?" The Sub-Inspector said, "We are not arresting you, we have been told to bring you in for questioning." Hariharan began to get angry and he said, "Oh really! Just for questioning, huh? And if I refuse?" The Sub-

Inspector immediately said, "Then we will have to arrest you!"

Hariharan flared up immediately and told him, "You come to my house at 6 o'clock in the morning and you threaten to arrest me without informing me of the reason for my arrest? Do you know what a police state is, or is anything that you do justified because I am a Dalit?" The Sub-Inspector said, "Sir, I am a Dalit myself!" Hariharan glared at him and almost shouted, "You too, Brutus!" He took a deep breath to calm himself and then told the Sub-Inspector, "I will need five minutes to throw on some proper clothes. You wait right here until I am dressed!" He was ready within the five minutes and went with the team to the police station.

Inspector Jamal and his Sub-Inspector, Govind, decided to first question Faisal. They were sitting in a small room which held just a table and four chairs. Faisal was brought in and seated in a chair at the table facing Jamal and Govind who sat across from him. Inspector Jamal waited for Faisal to say something but he didn't oblige and just sat and stared at him. Finally, Inspector Jamal asked him, "Do you know why you were brought in for questioning?" Faisal replied, "I am not an oracle, nor am I a mind reader. The people who arrested me refused to tell me the reason for my arrest, although I asked them." Sub-Inspector Govind said, "You are not under arrest; you have just been brought in for questioning." Faisal snorted and told him, "A rose by any other name is still a rose!" Inspector Jamal intervened smoothly and said, "But it is true, you know. We only want to question you and you have not been arrested."

Faisal sighed and told him, "Let's cut the crap. If I am not under arrest then I am free to leave." He stood up and Sub-Inspector Govind immediately said, "You cannot leave!" Faisal smiled at Inspector Jamal and sat down. "See?" he said. "As I was saying, you arrested me, so go ahead and ask your questions and I'll decide whether I want to answer them or not." Sub-Inspector Govind told him sharply, "If you refuse to answer our questions then we *will* arrest you!" Inspector Jamal made a downward movement of his hand to tell Govind to stop talking and then he told Faisal, "I just want to ask you a few questions regarding the Dalit village incident and the interview you gave to a television channel at that time." Faisal said, "Oh that? Well, I've already spoken to the police and David Joseph about that."

Sub-Inspector Govind said harshly, "Never mind what you told them! We want to know what you meant by saying that the same incident could happen on a larger scale with poison being used to contaminate the water supply. You said that only if this happened on a large scale could change happen for the benefit of the Dalits. So did you decide to make this happen? Did you decide to make the change happen?"

There was a look of surprise mixed with consternation on Faisal's face as he exclaimed, "You want to pin this poisoning on me?! Why? Because I'm a Muslim?" Inspector Jamal said, "No, because you are a Dalit activist. And we are not trying to pin anything on you, we are just questioning you." Faisal was angry and he said, "So, because I'm a Muslim *and* a Dalit activist, I automatically become a suspect? Go ahead and arrest me and let me see you prove anything against me!" Inspector Jamal tried to be conciliatory and he said, "Look, no one is accusing you of anything, we are just following up on some leads and we need to ask you a few questions and that is all."

But Faisal gave him an angry look and said, "This man has just now openly accused me, so I have nothing further to say. If you people can twist what I said in a television debate, then imagine what you can do with whatever I say here. Go ahead! Arrest me and I will have my day in court." Inspector Jamal asked him, "Are you willing to give me the passwords for your laptop and phones?" But Faisal refused to answer and stayed silent.

Inspector Jamal signalled to his Sub-Inspector and they left the room. When they were outside,

Jamal told him, “If you antagonise the ones we are questioning at the very start, then they will either refuse to talk or they will just lie. There is a difference in questioning a person against whom you have nothing more than a suspicion and questioning someone against whom you have some sort of evidence! I want you to just sit and learn and not talk. Is that understood?” Sub-Inspector Govind said, “I’m sorry Sir! Yes Sir!” Inspector Jamal called a woman constable and told her, “Ask the man inside if he would like something to drink or eat and provide what he asks for. Tell him I will talk to him again in half an hour and please make sure to be very, very polite when talking to him.”

They then sat in a similar room and questioned Hariharan. Inspector Jamal asked him, “After the incident at the Dalit village you spoke on a television channel and you sounded very angry.” Hariharan did not speak but just stared at him. Inspector Jamal continued and said, “During that interview you also said that the authorities were not taking the incident seriously just because it was a Dalit village. Isn’t that right?” Hariharan continued to stare at him and said, “What I have stated in that interview is in the public domain, so you have obviously seen the footage. So what is the purpose of asking me now if I have said it or not? Do you think that I am a moron to deny what I have said knowing full well that the footage is there for all to see?" Inspector Jamal again asked him, "But you were angry because you felt that the authorities were not taking the incident seriously enough. Isn't that right?" Hariharan said, "Of course I was angry! That was an inhuman act!"

Inspector Jamal agreed and said, "Yes, it was! You also said that if the same thing had happened elsewhere, perhaps in an upper caste village, then the authorities would have taken it more seriously." Hariharan shrugged and said, "I still believe that and I will continue to believe that until the time that Dalits are treated as equals, not just by society but also by the police and the authorities." Inspector Jamal remarked mildly, "But we *do* treat everyone as equals." Hariharan grimaced and said, "Don't spout the party line to me! That is what everyone says and claims, but the reality on the ground is different and I know it from personal experience!"

Inspector Jamal abruptly asked him in a harsh tone, "Where did you get the idea of contaminating the main water supply?" Hariharan gave him a steady look and said cautiously, "I'm tempted to react to that with sarcasm, but knowing you people and how you work, I hesitate to do so. Do you know why? Because you would take my sarcasm, misinterpret it, mix it in with ideology and my social activism, add a pinch of my hyperbole, sprinkle it with a little of your accusations and there you have it! The perfect recipe to arrest me for mass murder!" Inspector Jamal was irritated and told him, "I know that you are highly educated, but using big words does not answer my question!" Hariharan sighed and replied, "Because your question insinuates that I thought and plotted and came up with this idea for mass murder and therefore I am guilty of poisoning the water tank." Inspector Jamal almost shouted, "But you did come up with the idea!"

Hariharan said with exasperation, "Me and a hundred others I am sure! Are you saying that after that Dalit village incident, you people never thought of how easy it would be to replicate the same thing on a larger scale?" Before Inspector Jamal could say anything he continued, "Either you guys thought about it and did not bother to tighten security or you actually did not think of it! And I really don't know which is worse!"

Inspector Jamal spoke in a more normal tone and told him, "You were angry at what had taken place, you accused the authorities of not doing enough, you said that if this had happened somewhere else then the authorities would react immediately, and then you came up with the idea of contaminating a larger source of the water supply. So I am wondering if you then decided to prove what you claimed by creating the scenario that you spoke of." Hariharan gave him a resigned look and said, "Are you wondering or are you asking me?" Inspector Jamal said irritably, "I am asking you!" Hariharan replied shortly, "The answer is no!"

Inspector Jamal stared at him intently and said, "We are searching your house right now. Are you saying that we will not find anything to substantiate our claims? We are very thorough in what we do and when we search, we *really* search!" Hariharan told him sarcastically, "I bet you *really* search! I've heard the stories of planting evidence on laptops, creating false letters, messages, and what not. But let me tell you this! Outside of you planting evidence you will not find anything, and you can search until doomsday for all the good it will do you!" Inspector Jamal pounced on his words and said, "You are so sure that you have obliterated all evidence? Don't be so sure, because we are very good at finding what has been overlooked." Hariharan said fiercely, "This conversation is going nowhere! You will simply continue to twist anything that I say. All I am saying is that you won't find anything because there is nothing to find. I did not carry out this terrible act, but as you are obviously not going to believe me, I have nothing further to say. So go ahead and arrest me and let the actual criminal go scot-free." Inspector Jamal asked him, "Are you willing to give me the passwords for your laptop and phones?" But

Hariharan did not give him an answer. Inspector Jamal continued to question him but Hariharan just sat silent and refused to talk.

While Faisal and Hariharan were being questioned, teams of the central agencies were searching their houses, cars, laptops, and phones. They were also checking their bank accounts and tracing all payments made with debit and credit cards. They were searching to try and find a link to the purchase of arsenic trioxide and they were checking their bank accounts to see if they had received a sudden infusion of money which was not fully accounted for. They found a lot of literature about Dalits and Dalit icons on the laptops of both men. Neither of the two men's laptops were password protected and neither were their phones.

The Inspector in charge of the search teams phoned Jamal and told him, "Their laptops and their phones are not password protected, so I don't think we are going to find anything there." Jamal sighed and said, "Search everything anyway, and I'll get permission to check their social media accounts and will send the details to you as soon as I receive it." The Inspector said, "I'll do that, but are you sure that one of them is the guilty party? I'm only asking because with their phones and laptops being unprotected..." Jamal told him, "Right now we don't have any other leads so let's do a thorough check on these two and then we'll see. I'll keep them in holding here while we check out their bank accounts and also their social media accounts. Maybe we'll find something and then I can interrogate them again." He gave instructions that Hariharan and Faisal were to remain in holding. He told his Sub-Inspector Govind, "See that they have lunch as per their preferences and ensure that they have enough water. Provide toilet facilities whenever requested by them."

INTERVIEWS

MAY 18, TUESDAY - AFTERNOON

DAVID AND RAMYA

RAMYA AND DAVID reached the house of Prakash the writer around 1 o'clock in the afternoon. It was less than a half hour's drive from the house of Siva and Ramya commented, "Both of them actually live close enough to the contaminated water tank." The house was quite large, only a single floor, but with quite a large compound surrounding the house which was built right in the middle of the housing plot. The gate was locked but there was a calling bell at the side of the gate and David pressed it. He waited for a minute and then pressed it again, holding it this time for at least half a minute and they could hear the bell ringing somewhere in the house. After about five minutes David pressed the buzzer again and this time the front door opened almost immediately and a medium height, light-skinned man, who looked to be in his forties stood there and asked them, "Something I can do for you? If you're selling something, I'm not interested!"

Ramya moved in front of David, and on seeing her uniform the man immediately said, "Wait a minute!" He disappeared back into the house and came out again with a bunch of keys in his hand. He opened the gate and told them, "Come in please. Sorry about that, but I keep the gate locked because sales people and others looking for donations and whatnot just walk right in and then I have to waste my time talking to them. I'm usually very busy and don't like to be disturbed." He led the way into his house and seated them in a comfortably furnished sit-out. When they were seated he sat down and asked Ramya, "So what can I do to help the police?" He paused for a beat and then said with a smile, "That is of course if you're not here to arrest me!"

David told him, "We just wanted to talk to you about a television interview that you did after the Dalit village incident. As you know, a few days ago someone poisoned a large overhead water tank and many people are dead and seriously ill." Prakash said with a sombre look on his face, "Yes, I know about that, and to think that I had actually talked about such a thing happening at that interview!"

David asked him, “From that interview, I gathered that you had actually written a book about an event like this of mass poisoning?” Prakash gave him a rueful smile and said, “If you watched that interview then you know that the book was never published. But I wrote that book after I had written an article that spoke about the lack of security around our water supply and the dangers inherent in that lack of security.”

David asked him, “And was that article well received?” Prakash shook his head and said, “No, I don’t think anyone bothered because I couldn’t find any signs of the security being tightened. No one listened and so I wrote a book hoping that it would get someone’s attention. But there! No one was even interested in publishing it!” David told him, “Maybe that was because another writer named Siva had already written a book on the same subject?” Prakash shrugged and said, “I know the book that Siva wrote, but that was about poison being dumped in a dam, and well...” He didn’t complete the sentence so David prompted him, “And...?” Prakash grimaced and said hesitatingly, “Well...I don’t like to comment on the work of another writer, but you know, dumping poison in a large dam and so many people dying as a result...well...not quite believable...or realistic let us say.”

David asked him, “So your story was different in

what way? I read a lot, you know, and I'm always interested in the contrasting approach that different writers take for a similar storyline!" Prakash sat up a bit and said, "Well, my book was very realistic. It was about poison being dumped in an overhead tank that distributes water to different localities!" David exclaimed, "So! Exactly like how it happened now, and yet they refused to publish it? You must be feeling really vindicated now!" Prakash squared his shoulders and told David, "Just imagine if my book had been published or if they had at least paid attention to the article I wrote, then this catastrophe could have been avoided!" His eyes lit up and his face had a fierce look, but when he spoke again his voice was calm. "I suppose I should feel vindicated, but I feel sad that such a thing had to happen for the authorities to wake up to the danger. But there it is, we are always reactive instead of being proactive."

David said with some feeling, "You must have been furious when they refused to publish your book! I know I would have been very angry if I was in your place." Prakash said, "Well, you know, rejection is part and parcel of the life of a writer." But David persisted and said animatedly, "Yes of course! But when someone writes something that's so *meaningful* for society as a whole, pointing out the *dangers* that we face while we go about our lives blissfully unaware of what might happen! At least then you would expect to find people who would value such writing! But what did they do? They rejected your work!"

As David was speaking, Prakash's face started to take on a darker hue and his eyes had an intense look. His hands slowly turned into fists and when David had finished he thumped his fists on his thighs and almost growled, "*You* can recognise that, but did the others? Oh no! They think they are the smart ones, just because they can turn down your work! I tried to explain to so many people what the purpose of the book was, but did they listen? Hah!!" David raised his voice slightly and asked him, "And the purpose of the book was?" Prakash instantly replied, "To point out the dangers that exist right in front of us! The police are always looking for bombs and guns and whatnot, but then there is something like this that is staring them in the face and yet they just cannot see it!" Still keeping his voice slightly raised, David told him, "Now the police are saying that this is just the work of a madman and no one could have seen it coming!"

Prakash's features became contorted with rage and he almost shouted, "They never listen! So many smart people have warned about similar dangers but they never listen! Even now they are not listening I can tell you!" David suddenly spoke mildly and said, "They have tightened up security so what makes you think that they are not listening now?" With an almost physical effort Prakash calmed down and said, "I heard on the news that they have arrested those two men who are Dalit social activists, just because they had also suggested somewhat the same thing as I did on those television debates."

David asked him, "After that television interview did anyone speak to you about what you had said. Did anyone comment on the feasibility of what you said? Did anyone comment on your article or on your book?" Prakash's mind seemed far away and he just stared blankly at David, but then with a shake of his head as though to bring his mind back to the present he said, "I'm not sure, but even if someone had commented on it, why would that matter?" David shrugged and told him, "I don't think it matters. It's just that some of the others who spoke on similar lines during those debates received a phone call from an anonymous caller who praised them for what they had spoken about. This caller even praised Siva's novel!"

Prakash frowned and stared down at the floor for a long moment. Suddenly he looked up at David and said, "Wait, wait! A phone call? Now why didn't I remember that? Yes, I did get a phone call and the caller said that he agreed with what I had said during that interview." David asked him, "Do you remember the day that you got that call? Go back to that interview in your mind and think of something that caught your attention after the interview. Then think of something important that happened the next day, something that you definitely remember. Then move on to the next day and again think of what may have happened on that day. That's a method that the other people used and they remembered the day and the time of the call. If you concentrate and do the same, I'm sure you will remember the day you got that call."

Prakash frowned again while he thought and he began licking his lips and rubbing his mouth. Finally, he said, "I'm sure it was two days after that interview and it would have been between 3 o'clock to 4 o'clock in the afternoon." David told him, "That's really good the way you can remember that! The day *and* the time!" Prakash shrugged and said, "I just did what you suggested and it seems to have worked." David told him, "Now I want you to try and remember the exact words that the caller said. You've proven that you have a good memory and I'm sure that you will recall the exact words." Prakash again frowned and asked him, "Why do the exact words matter?"

David shrugged and told him, "I don't know if it matters or not, I'm just trying to see if the caller used the same words to all the people." Then he added, "Siva remembered the exact words that the caller said." Prakash again took his time and then he said, "Yes, yes, I think I remember now! He said, 'You were spot on with your book. That was very well written and something like that is bound to happen but ignorant people will never really see what is right in front of their faces! Siva's book was good too, but it can't happen like that and I'm sure the end is wrong where he talks about drones.' Then he cut the call."

David asked him, "You didn't think the call was strange at the time?" Prakash frowned and said, "No, it was after the interview and so I thought it was someone who had watched the programme. Besides, I just thought that he was comparing both the books. You know, Siva's book and mine." He paused for a moment and then added, "Even now as I think of it, I don't find anything strange. Again, I ask you, is that call important?" David shrugged and said, "I don't really know to be honest! I'm just following whatever leads I can find. By the way, you were talking in the beginning about the police questioning Faisal and Hariharan. Does that upset you?" Prakash gave him a wry smile and said, "Well, they could come for me next! But they're fools! Surely they don't think that those two social activists did something like this?" David asked him, "You mean you don't think social activists can carry out acts of terror?"

Prakash grew angry and said, "You're talking the language of the police, of course! Before, they thought that this wasn't feasible, and now they think it is an act of terror? But before this you said that they think a madman did this!" David smiled and told him, "So you do have a good memory! Yes, the police think a madman must have done this but they are also looking into the terror angle." Prakash said grimly, "The only angle they should be looking at is the security angle! That's what I was trying to get the authorities to recognise when I wrote about this; the lack of security. I don't think even now they are listening and recognising the danger that surrounds us." David stared at him for a moment longer and then stood up. "Thanks for taking the time to talk to us," he said. Prakash also stood up and said, "Well, let's hope the authorities are taking security seriously now. And if they want to come for me next, well, here I am so let them come! I will be ready and willing to answer them!"

David and Ramya drove back to Raj's house, because David told her, "Let's go and sit down and sift through all the interviews we have done and then I'll hopefully see my way clear."

PRAKASH

After they had gone, Prakash paced the floor of his sitting room with his head bent, staring at the floor as he walked. 'So the police were questioning everyone who had spoken about such an event at those television interviews,' he thought. 'Well, questioning everyone was all right, but arresting those two activists? That shows that the police are still not willing to admit that there is a danger of a terrorist attack on our water supply.' He frowned as he paced the floor and aloud he said, "When will they learn to listen to people who are smart enough to recognise the danger that exists in front of us?" He shook his head and thought, 'It's almost as though they are waiting for something worse to happen before they will really open their eyes and see the truth.'

Prakash had an easy life growing up. He was an only child, and his parents were both well-educated and held good jobs, and he had never wanted for anything. He had gone to college and completed his degree in engineering. He had landed a well-paying job, and he had worked as an engineer for nearly ten years. But then he had suddenly discovered a love for writing. One day he had seen an advertisement for a writing contest, and he had made a spur-of-the-moment decision to enter it. He happened to be bored at the time with nothing to do, and he thought it might be amusing to try something totally out of his field of engineering. But when he started to write, he found that the words and ideas flowed freely, and when he had finished the article, he felt a sense of satisfaction that he had never felt before. He did not win that contest, but he found that it did not matter to him. He began writing short stories and then articles for newspapers, and finally he wrote a book. The book got published and did reasonably well in sales. After that, he forgot about engineering and became a full-time writer.

Gradually, his focus in writing shifted to realism, and he began to write about the slums, about the pollution of the rivers, and about the gangsters in the big cities. Then he wrote a book about the effects of terrorism on the lives of ordinary people, and it was then that he became interested in the security aspect of essential things like the potable water supply. He was very excited when he had finished the book, and then came the rejections. No one believed the story, and that is when he became fixated on the subject!

ANALYSIS

MAY 18, TUESDAY -
AFTERNOON TO NIGHT

DAVID AND RAMYA

WHEN THEY WERE SEATED in the room at Raj's house, Ramya told David, "From what I can gather, everyone is fixated on something or the other." She thought for a bit and then added, "Except for Swarna, she doesn't seem to be fixated on anything, except of course for the environment. By the way, I did some research on each of these people, and Swarna lived in a slum area until she was about nine years old." David interrupted and remarked, "So that would explain why she is an environmental activist." Ramya continued, "She went to college on a full scholarship and majored in environmental science and technology." David said, "So she is intelligent, and with her background, the environment obviously means a lot to her."

He rubbed his chin while he thought for a while, and then he asked her, "What about Rajesh the political analyst?" Ramya said, "Well, not really any obsession I suppose, but he does seem fixated on the idea of someone doing something to give the government a bad name, and as I said, he does belong to the opposite side in politics." David gave her his phone and told her, "I've recorded all the conversations we have had with all these persons of interest, so download it to your laptop, and you can listen to them once again." Ramya raised her eyebrows in surprise and said, "But you didn't get their permission, so isn't that illegal?"

David shrugged and told her, "So sue me! I'm not the police, and when I go after a criminal, I'm not concerned with the nuances of the law. Besides, I'm not going to use this for anything illegal, and it's not for me but for you. I always remember everything that is said when I interview someone, but I wanted something to refresh your recollection so that you will be able to give me your take on things that were said." Ramya rubbed her nose and said, "But if you had asked them, I am sure that they would not have objected." David did not answer her, and after a while, she said, "But they would have been guarded in what they spoke!" David gave her a silent clap and said, "Good for you! Now download that and listen to it, and then we'll talk."

While Ramya was downloading the recordings from the phone, David pulled out his notebook and was reading what he had written down. Ramya asked him, "What's that?" David looked up and said, "After any interview or conversation, I have this habit of jotting down notes on what was said and my impressions at the time. It helps me later on when I'm looking at the whole picture." Ramya looked surprised and asked him, "You mean you don't use a computer?" David smiled and replied, "I do in fact! Once a week I enter everything from my notebook, with expansions and added notes, into my computer. But that is just for a record that I keep on all my cases. Many times, similar things happen, and then I can refer back to a previous case."

He paused in thought and then told her, "But the computer I use for my records has no connection to the internet via email or anything else that could be hacked." Ramya asked him, "It's good to be careful, but were you hacked at any time?" David said grimly, "Yes, I was! A psychopath used an email to plant a virus in my computer, and he got the names of people who were involved in some of my cases, and he went after them to get at me. I've been extremely careful after that event!"

Ramya looked interested and asked him, "Was

that the same case that Hari was mentioning when he spoke about a house of horrors?" But David told her, "No, that was the case of those two psychopaths. Hari had entered the house when both of them were out, and what he found was a cellar of horrors! The psychopath who later targeted me was the brother of one of those men. He was very shrewd and intelligent, and after his brother was arrested, he had decided to pit his wits against mine. At that time, none of us knew that one of the psychopaths had a brother." Ramya was now very intrigued and asked him, "And the email you were just talking about?" David told her, "He was a master of the subtle disguise. He joined a class I was holding for student psychologists, claiming that he was writing a book about a psychopath and that the lessons would be invaluable to him. I later learned from the students that he had actually befriended some of them and that it was he who had come up with the idea of me holding a class for the students. He then offered to do a lot of the routine work, like printing out copies of my lectures, etc. and made himself kind of indispensable. He used to send me emails because I would send the material to be printed to him via email. That's how he inserted a virus and was able to see all my records of past cases."

Ramya exclaimed, "And then he targeted them!" David told her, "He targeted them to send a challenge to me. You know, kind of a catch-me-if-you-can challenge. But one of the victims died, an innocent young girl, and two were tortured before we caught him." Ramya was shocked, and she said, "That must have been a terrible time! No wonder Raj, Hari, and you are so close." David was thoughtful when he told her, "Yes, Raj, of course, has been my best friend since our schooldays. We were both interested in crime, but he always wanted to be a policeman, and I always wanted to be a psychologist. After my parents died, he married my sister. But you know, even in bad times, there is always some good. That psychopath was targeting people I knew, and my wife Rani and her two daughters were on that list. Of course, at that time, we weren't married, but we were seeing each other. To protect her, I convinced her to move into my house with her two daughters because my house had round-the-clock security. That was how we became closer, and finally, she agreed to marry me."

Suddenly he smiled and said, "In fact, that is how my younger stepdaughter met her future husband and that is how Hari met and fell in love with my elder stepdaughter Devika and married her. Hari was in charge of their security and accompanied them whenever they had to leave the house." He paused for a moment and then added, "Anyway, after that I've been extremely careful that no one can access my records." Ramya was so engrossed in listening to him that when he stopped speaking, she still just sat and stared at him as though expecting to hear more. David snapped his fingers and said with a smile, "Ramya, the recordings?" She started up in surprise and then shook her head as though to clear it. "I would love to hear about all your cases," she told him. David smiled and said, "Maybe sometime, but right now shall we get back to work?"

Ramya had finished the download, and she now played the recording of the interview with Swarna. After listening to it, David told her, "Right there at the beginning when she was a bit agitated thinking that we might suspect her, she said something that interested me." Ramya had been using voice recognition software to get the recording transcribed as they were listening to it, and now she read the beginning of the transcript. After a while, she remarked, "She did say something about polluting water bodies, that it would take a catastrophe for people to learn." But David said, "Before that, she said that she had nothing to do with this latest attack." Ramya frowned and stared at the transcript while she thought. Then suddenly she looked up and said, "This *latest* attack! That's it, isn't it?"

David smiled at her and said, "Now you're really getting into this! Normally a person would just say that she had nothing to do with *this* attack. By saying this *latest* attack, it shows that her mind is very much on the previous Dalit village incident. Now it can mean that she had nothing to do with this latest attack but had or knew something about the previous attack. That's what I meant when I told you that you have to listen to what people say and their facial expressions and eyes when they speak about different things. If you want to know what's on a person's mind then it's the nuances that count."

Ramya asked him, "And in this case?" David shrugged and said, "In this case it means nothing because I had just spoken about the previous incident and connected it to this attack, and so it most probably was just an association of those thoughts. In the beginning, she had stated *this* attack." Ramya nodded and said, "You're just teaching me what to look for, I get it." David told her, "But you did get to the relevant fact immediately when you picked out what she said about a catastrophe. That is the thinking that drives many eco-terrorists to commit such acts of terror!" Ramya remarked, "They want to save the environment, and they believe that the ends justify the means. Yes, that is why I provoked her with that question."

David rubbed his chin and then said, "Put her down as a possible for now. She *is* very angry about the pollution of water bodies!" Ramya asked him, "So this is essentially an exercise to eliminate or separate suspects based on probabilities?" David explained it to her and said, "You put down pros and cons against each person, and then you start to narrow down the field based on probabilities, whether they have the means, whether they were present at the time or maybe they could have an accomplice, things like that. Once you've separated the chaff from the grain, then it becomes easier to concentrate on what remains, and you will get a breakthrough." Ramya said, "So she is a definite possible?" But David replied, "I doubt it, just a possible I think for now." Ramya was curious, and she told him, "But you don't think she did it."David shrugged and said, "She is a well-grounded person. I am looking for someone with an obsession. She is concerned and angry at what is happening to the environment, but to me, she doesn't seem obsessed by it."

They then listened to the conversation with Rajesh the political analyst. Ramya remarked, "He again brought up the idea of a psycho being responsible for this just to embarrass the government. He seemed pretty sure that this wasn't a terrorist attack but the act of an individual." David asked her, "So what do you think?" She thought about it and then told him, "I would eliminate him." David said, "Tell me why you would eliminate him as a suspect." She rubbed her nose and then said, "He is definitely not obsessed with the idea of someone doing something to embarrass the government. As for saying that this definitely was not the act of a terror cell but rather the act of a lone psycho, well, to me it just shows that he's pretty smart at analysing things." David agreed and told her, "He is a political analyst, so coming to that conclusion would be quite natural for him, and yes, he does not appear to be obsessed with the idea of embarrassing the government. That's just part of his job to think up ways that may affect politics. If he is connected to this attack, then it must be through a person to whom he had spoken about this idea. Maybe he spoke to a party member? If he did, he is definitely not going to admit it, and so we can never find out for certain. But I'm sure he is not directly connected, so go ahead and eliminate him."

Ramya then listened to the conversation with Hariharan, and she said, "I wonder what the police have against him. They must have some kind of evidence or trail for them to arrest him." David told her, "Forget about the central agencies! I can tell you that if it had been up to Raj, then he wouldn't have arrested either Hariharan or Faisal. Not without proof, and the agencies don't have any proof." Ramya stared at him and then said, "You seem very sure of that. Why do you think that they don't have any proof?" David said, "Let's be logical about this.

What proof is possible in a case like this? The agencies are looking for a money trail, but that would only exist if the perpetrator belonged to a terror cell. How are you going to establish a money trail for an individual buying poison?"

Ramya said, "Well, credit card or debit card usage in places where you can get arsenic trioxide for a start, and..." She hesitated and then stopped and sighed. "I get what you are saying," she told David. "He wouldn't have used a card; he would have used cash." David prompted her, "And...?" She rubbed her nose and said, "He would have bought small quantities at a time, and he would have stretched his purchases over a long period of time as well. He would have bought the stuff using false names and maybe using simple disguises as you told me. Yes, I agree there would be no trail."

David then told her, "Actually, in these types of cases, there *will* be a trail, but you will find that trail and the necessary proof only *after* you have identified the criminal. That's the difference in cases of this type." Ramya told him, "So the agencies have no proof, but they are...what was it you told Inspector Jamal? A bull in a china shop!" David told her, "Arsenic trioxide is used in the manufacture of glass and wood furniture. As I told you, it would be quite simple for this man to strike up an acquaintance with a small manufacturer and get him to part with a small amount of the stuff by perhaps claiming that he was making a trial run to see if he should get into the business or something along those lines. There are so many ways to get this stuff that it would astonish the public if they knew about it!" Ramya was curious and asked him, "You've come across cases of arsenic poisoning before this then?" David sighed and said, "Yes, quite a few times, I would say."

Ramya said, "So what do you think about Hariharan? I think he should be eliminated from the list. You said that he even felt guilty about his success and that is why he is working as an activist for his community. You said that was the guilt of a good man." David shook his head and told her, "But that guilt could easily turn into an obsession to finally bring about a change for his community. Don't forget that he has suffered a great trauma as a teenager, so he has personal experience of what the caste system can do. The human mind is much more fragile than we think, and the best among us can do the worst with the best of intentions. It is so easy to justify anything to yourself if you want to." Ramya gave him an exasperated look and said, "So is psychology just a way of saying yes *and* no for anything and everything?"

David laughed and said, "I understand your confusion, believe me. You have to really study the subject and get enough hands-on or practical experience before you can truly understand and use psychology as a tool. The human mind is so complex and devious that even an experienced and gifted psychologist can be fooled at times!" Turning serious, he told her, "That psychopath who targeted me had me fooled completely in the beginning. He was perfectly normal and eager to help out in any way because I had agreed to his joining that class. I have told you before this that a true psychopath can interact and appear completely normal in everyday life. They learn to mimic the human emotions of compassion and kindness."

Changing the subject, he told her, "Criminal psychology is a fascinating subject, although hard to master fully. But I think you have the gift for it. You would make a good psychologist." Ramya shook her head and said, "Anyway, back to Hariharan. I don't think he is obsessed with anything. I think he is sincere in trying to do the best for his community. Yes, he gets angry. But as you said, he is short-tempered, and while that is not good for a relationship, it has nothing to do with being obsessed. So I say we eliminate him from the list."

David told her in his sympathetic voice, "Someone close to you was short-tempered." She looked at him in surprise, and he explained, "There was a slight change in your voice and your facial expression when you mentioned relationships." She sighed and said, "Yes, in college I was going steady with a nice guy, but his short temper was something that really spoilt that relationship, so I ended it." He asked her in his calm, soothing voice, "You loved him?" She thought for a moment and then said, "In the beginning, I thought I was in love with him, but I soon realised that it is very hard to love a man with such a short temper." She paused for a moment and then added, "The best way that I can explain it is this: it was like walking across a field of buried landmines. You have to be alert all the time because you never know when you might set one off!"

David was silent, and finally she shook her head and said, "But enough of that. Let's get back to the here and now. Shall we eliminate Hariharan?" David agreed but said, "Yes, I think we can eliminate him, but put a question mark next to his name." Ramya was surprised and asked him, "Why the question mark?" David told her, "That man is in need of counselling, and once this is over, I intend to give him the name of a good man who is excellent in anger management." Suddenly he said, "I wonder how Inspector Jamal is getting along with questioning him. Hariharan has a very sharp tongue, and he has the erudition to back it up!"

Ramya next pulled up the interview with Faisal. She said, "The point in his favour is that he wasn't here at all but in Chennai for the previous ten days.

We checked, and his story is true." Suddenly she said, "I wonder if Inspector Jamal knows about that?" David shrugged and said, "Even if he was in Chennai, he could have had an accomplice who carried out the crime, so that won't carry any weight with Inspector Jamal." Ramya stared at him and said, "Is that what you think?" But David shrugged and replied, "That's what Inspector Jamal will think. So tell me what you think of Faisal, the pros and cons." Ramya was reading the transcript, and suddenly she said with a mischievous smile, "Well, one thing in his favour is that he recognised *the* David Joseph!" David laughed and then told her, "There are times when you remind me so much of my younger stepdaughter, Revathi. But go on, the pros and cons."

Turning serious again, Ramya said, "Besides the fact that he wasn't here but in Chennai, he just didn't seem to be an obsessive kind of person. To me, he appeared quite rational, although I am aware that your profile states that the person responsible could be quite rational except where his obsession is concerned. But if Faisal is obsessed, then he has to be obsessed about the injustice to Dalits and the poor because that is what he is focused on. Yes, when he spoke about the incident in the Dalit village, he sounded angry, but I felt that he was more anguished than angry over it."

David told her, “You should seriously think about going back to college and studying psychology. It would be a huge asset even in your present profession. But yes, I agree with you about Faisal. Even when he spoke about catastrophes bringing about change, it wasn’t just his theory or idea that he was speaking about; it was history. There was no ‘I’ in what he was saying, just the bare fact that history shows us that catastrophes and calamities force people to effect a change in society.”

Ramya asked him, “I’m curious about that, so could you give me an example? I mean, even the pandemic only made us change our ways for a short time, and now we’re back to square one!” David said, “I’ll give you a great historic example: the Great London Fire of the 1600s! It forced the authorities to plan a better city with better sanitation and working conditions. Before the fire, London was swept by the Great Plague, and nothing could be done about it because of the crowded and unsanitary conditions that people were forced to live and work in. Until then, the authorities were not bothered about the living conditions of the people, and most buildings were made of wood and other combustible materials, and there was no proper sanitation to speak of, but the fire changed all that. So a great catastrophe brought about better living conditions for the poor and working people and better housing and sanitation."

Ramya remarked, "So it was in that context that Faisal spoke about change." She thought for a moment and then said, "I believe we can eliminate his name from the list. By the way, Faisal comes from a wealthy Muslim family. They own a chain of departmental stores, but he prefers to concentrate on his social activism." David agreed with her that he could be eliminated, and she then pulled the next recording, which was that of Siva the writer.

After listening to the conversation again, Ramya said, "If I had to pick someone, then this is the guy that I would pick! He is definitely obsessed, he is delusional, he expects everyone to listen to him and admire his genius, and anyone who doesn't listen is stupid!" David was rubbing his chin while he thought, and now he said, "Yes, he is definitely one of my top suspects, but not for the reasons that you just mentioned." Ramya was surprised and said, "But he is definitely obsessed with himself and his writing and thoughts. If anyone disagrees with him, then they are stupid. You had to struggle to get a word in because he just wouldn't stop talking about himself! He was happy about the phone call simply because the caller said he was brilliant. I would say that if you're looking for obsession, then he's a prime candidate!"

David told her, "Tell me the one word that he used the most during our conversation, or rather, one word that stood out!" Ramya frowned and read the transcript again. She was rubbing her nose, which David now understood to be her mannerism when she was deep in thought. Suddenly her eyes opened wide, and she looked up and exclaimed, "His mother!" David agreed and told her, "Read that transcript carefully. He wasn't so angry at the reactions to his book, but his mother was. He feels vindicated now because, quote, 'they will have to eat their words.' But that is what his mother said, not what he thought or said. Everything comes down to his mother, even remembering the time of the phone call because his mother got angry that he was eating late."

Ramya was keenly listening to him and reading the transcript at the same time, and now she said, "Yes, yes, I am seeing that now as I read the transcript. He is totally under his mother's thumb. But again I say that to me he is an obsessed person, and I have no doubt about that." David agreed but told her, "He is obsessed to prove to the world, and through them, hopefully, his mother, that he is capable and brilliant on his own merits. His mother has made him believe that everything he is, is because of her. I have seen this so often in so many of my patients. She has slowly but steadily robbed him of his self-esteem, so that now everything he says has to be on the lines of what his mother says or thinks."

He thought for a moment and then said, "I wouldn't be surprised if his mother gave him the idea of writing that book, and I think she got the idea from the article that Mahesh had written. That was the first article on this subject, and then came Siva's book and then Prakash's article and then Prakash's book, so I wouldn't be surprised if she gave him the idea in the first place to write that book."

Suddenly Ramya said, "Come to think of it, when he was rambling on and on, I stood up and spoke sternly to him, and he became more subdued!" David told her, "That is because of his conditioning. He has always been subdued by his mother. If you listen to the audio again, I took the hint from you, and when he again tried to ramble on, I cut him off and spoke sternly to him, and he immediately complied. He shouts at others and tries to take command of a conversation simply because he cannot do that with his mother." Ramya looked at him thoughtfully and then said, "But that would mean he does not fit your profile, because his obsession is to prove to his mother that he is better than she thinks." David just looked at her and said, "He does fit the profile. But go on and take what you're thinking to its proper conclusion and see what you can come up with." Ramya rubbed her nose and frowned. Then she said, as though she was talking to herself, "He wants to prove to his mother that he is better than she thinks he is. The book is not well received, and the sales were average, and that he feels is his failure again, so how does he prove his worth to his mother?" She suddenly looked at David in surprise and exclaimed, "Of course! He will try to make his story come true! Then he will be a great man to the public, and he will be free of his mother's control!"

David again applauded her with a silent clap and said, "That is good! Take my advice and go back to college. You have the mind for this profession." Ramya looked pleased at his praise but told him, "That will never happen because I can't afford to quit my job and go back to college. Both my parents are no more, and there is only my sister and myself." She looked very sad when she continued and told him, "She is married, and she had a daughter who I was very fond of. She died last year in a car accident with both my parents. She was just four years old, and it took me a long time to get over it." David commiserated with her but then told her, "Priya and I also lost our parents in a car crash when I was about your age. But if you decide to go back to college, then I can get you a full scholarship that will take care of everything. My younger stepdaughter,

Revathi, is married to Abhijeet Anand, and she is a social worker whose sole aim in life is to help women who have no one to turn to. They have a trust that gives a full scholarship to deserving women who cannot fulfil their dreams because of a lack of finance. You certainly fit that bill!" She was thoughtful, and David said, "You think about it, and after this is over, we will talk about it again."

THE SECOND ATTACK

MAY 18, TUESDAY - AFTERNOON TO NIGHT

THE MAN

IT TOOK the Man nearly two hours to change the appearance of his scooter. When he had thought out this plan of action, he had realised that using his scooter could be dangerous. He had used his scooter for dumping the arsenic in the sump of the overhead tank, but that was at midnight and he had obscured the licence plates with mud. But what he planned to do now had to be done just after dusk when everyone would be outside trying to enjoy whatever coolness there was to be had in the evening after a sweltering day. That he would be seen by many people was a given, so what he had to ensure was that what they saw would in no way lead back to him. There was no alternative to using his scooter as he had seen the men who used foggers for mosquitoes driving by slowly on a moped or a scooter. The fog machine was fixed to the vehicle and the spout was always horizontal. He, however, was going to point the spout upwards at an angle of more than 45 degrees in order to get the maximum dispersion.

His first plan to put arsenic in the sump of the overhead tank was simple, with hardly any danger to himself, and he had carried it out without any problem. The only difficult part of that plan was the procuring of the arsenic, but he had achieved that by being patient and had finally succeeded over a period of more than three months. But this second plan that he had conceived was more difficult and fraught with danger in the execution. He already had the arsenic, but he had to engineer a little adjustment to the fog machine to convert the arsenic into a gas. He also intended to release a very fine spray that would spread and settle down, thus making it more lethal. The gas would get into the lungs and the particles would settle on the skin and maybe even be ingested to some extent. It would also come in contact with the eyes. The danger lay in carrying out the plan. It had to be done just after dusk in full view of everyone, he had to use his own scooter, and he had to drive the scooter himself.

He had told himself that he was indeed brilliant

to conceive a plan like this. People were used to seeing a man in khaki clothing from the corporation driving along the road with the fog machine fixed to his moped. The sound of the approaching fog machine would make most people turn aside and immediately make their way indoors until the vehicle had passed by. He thought it was ironic that people became so used to seeing something that they didn't really *see* it anymore. He thought it was ironic because here he was trying to prove to the authorities that they weren't really *seeing* the danger that stared them in the face.

He stood in his backyard and felt the slight coolness from the evening breeze. If the wind increased, he thought, he would not carry out his plan today. Right now the breeze was just right to carry the particles over a large area, whereas if the wind became too strong then the particles and the gas would be dispersed far too quickly to have any real impact. He had now completed the work on his scooter. He had previously cut out shapes from a large sheet of thin plastic which he had painted black many days ago. The shapes fit the contours of the side panels of his scooter as well as the front panel. He had now stuck them carefully to the panels of his scooter. His scooter was a light blue colour and now the plastic sheets turned it to black. He had taken pains to make sure that the plastic shapes were stuck firmly and smoothly onto the scooter panels as it would not do for one of them to come loose and start flapping as he was driving along the road. He had prepared two fake licence plates and he now removed the original plates from his scooter and screwed on the fake ones. He stood back and regarded his work with satisfaction. He could now use his scooter safely because any description given to the police would not lead back to him.

He had also dug a pit at the back of the shed and had covered it with a thin concrete slab, such that the slab was level with the rest of the floor. He had then placed the large drum over it which concealed most of the slab. Today, after he had completed his plan, he would come back and dump the fog machine, fake licence plates, plastic sheets, and the containers used for the powder and acid into the pit. He would then cover everything over with the mud that he had collected and kept in two sacks, leaving a gap of about two feet between the mud and the top of the pit. He would then place the concrete slab over the pit and move the drum over the slab. '*It will take a genius to find it, he thought, but I'm better than anyone that the authorities have!*' He would also prepare a little surprise for the police if they did come calling. He smiled at the thought, and at that moment he looked completely insane although he did not know it!

He fitted the fog machine at the back of his scooter with clamps and cord that he had already prepared and tested so he knew that it would not come loose as he was driving. Now he went inside the house to get dressed. He wore the khaki clothing and pulled on a peaked cap so that most of his upper face was hidden. He put on a surgical mask like the ones everyone used during the pandemic and that obscured the rest of his face. Since the pandemic, no one noticed or commented if anyone wore a mask as many people still wore a mask in public. Now he was ready, he thought, as he regarded himself in the mirror. He was sure that no one could give a proper description to the police that would lead back to him, because he could hardly recognise himself now as he stared at his image in the mirror.

He had listened to all the discussions on the news channels as to the possible reasons for the three areas of Ram Nagar, Anbu Nagar, and Vivek Nagar, being chosen for such a terrible terror attack. He had laughed at their stupidity, because he knew that he had not selected any specific areas. He had chosen the large main overhead tank simply because it was the only one close enough of its type that covered a lot of localities. It was just fate or chance that the day after he had dumped the poison the water was released to those three areas. But for this attack he *had* chosen an area. He knew that the previous three affected areas would still be under tight security and people would be wary and on their guard, so he did not plan to release the poison there this time. He had chosen an area that was about five kilometres from where he lived. He had driven along those roads twice to make sure that he knew the layout perfectly. He had gone there during the day and then he had gone there again after the sun had set, to make sure that he would recognise the route that he would take even in the dark.

This was important because he had no intention of inhaling the poison himself. He had mapped out his route thoroughly. He would enter at one point and drive along without retracing his path so that he would not come in contact with the poisonous particles that were being spewed from the back of his scooter. He had also taken into account the direction of the wind. At this time of the year, the direction was constant and so his route would begin furthest away from the wind direction and he would work his way through the connecting streets towards the wind, thereby eliminating the possibility of the wind carrying the particles towards him. Of course, if the wind did suddenly change direction then he would simply switch off the fog machine and go home.

He was ready now and darkness had just taken

over the land, so he wheeled his scooter from the backyard to his gate. Before exiting his gate, he glanced all around to make sure that the road was deserted and that no one was outside their houses. This was the moment of greatest danger when someone might see him coming out of his house on a black scooter. The area outside his house was dark since he had not switched on the outside lights and that reduced the risk of him being seen. There was also no street light near his gate. Satisfying himself that he was not being observed, he wheeled his scooter out of his gate. He just shut the gate without locking it so that he could enter swiftly on his return without having to stop and unlock the gate. He got onto his scooter and drove silently away on his mission of death. Even now, if anyone had told him that he was insane, he would have laughed in their faces and told them that the insane ones were the people who would not listen when he had warned them about the dangers of the lack of security.

SILENT TERROR

MAY 18, TUESDAY - LATE EVENING

SHANTHI NAGAR

FATIMA WAS STANDING by her gate and talking to Geetha, who had been married for just eight months and lived across the road from her house. Fatima knew Geetha's husband well as they had been neighbours for nearly ten years now, but within a month of meeting Geetha she had grown fond of the young woman who was so full of life and loved to joke and laugh. She knew that Geetha was now three months pregnant and she never failed to give her daily warnings of all the things that she should be careful of during her pregnancy. Fatima was noted in the neighbourhood for her fetish about contamination and pollution. Geetha had crossed the road and was standing at Fatima's gate talking to her when they heard the sound of the approaching fog machine. "Don't these people usually come in the mornings or early in the evenings?" Fatima asked Geetha who shrugged and replied, "Maybe because the mosquitoes seem to have increased lately, especially late in the evenings." Fatima said, "Well, it's good to see that the corporation is doing its work. But let's go inside now or we'll be inhaling that smoke." Geetha laughed and told her, "Okay, but you do know that it is not harmful to humans."

Fatima turned to go into her house and said over her shoulder, "Maybe, and maybe bats are not harmful either, but I don't believe in taking chances. I'll see you later. Please go inside and shut your doors and windows. You should be extra careful now that you are bringing a new life into this world!" She went into her house and shut the front door and the windows so that the smoke wouldn't enter the house. Her daughter Sophia complained, "Mother! It's been such a hot day and now that it has turned a bit cool in the evening you are locking up everything?" Fatima shook her finger at her daughter and admonished her, "You won't melt! I'll open the windows after that smoke clears away." Sophia grumbled to herself, not realising at the time that her mother's concerns over health and pollution would spare their lives that day.

Geetha was laughing as she left Fatima and went into her house. Her husband, who had just come back from work and was watching television in the sitting room, asked her, "What's the joke?" She told him, "Nothing really, just old Fatima getting worried about the smoke for the mosquitoes. She also mentioned the bats! After the pandemic she never fails to tell everyone at every opportunity that the virus came from bats. She's such a nice old lady, but she always distrusts everything where health is concerned. Do you know that they will only drink boiled water in her house because she distrusts the water filters?" Her husband was watching the news and he just grunted and said, "Nowadays it seems wise to distrust most things. Have you forgotten about what happened on Friday to those poor people in Ram Nagar and the other two places?" Geetha started to laugh, but then suddenly sobered down as a flicker of fear ran through her mind. She did remember what had happened to those poor people on Friday. *'Imagine the water supply being poisoned,'* she thought! She suddenly closed and bolted the front door and then went and locked all the windows just as the man on his scooter went past with the fog machine making its dreadful noise. Thanks to Fatima and her neurosis, Geetha and her husband would survive that terrible night and so would the child in her womb.

Two streets further down, Muthu and Raja would not be so lucky. They were bachelors and they lived in a small rented house together. They had come back from work and they were in the small sitting room having a drink with the front door left wide open for the slightly cool evening breeze. They heard the sound of the fog machine and Muthu started to get up saying, “Damn! Now the smoke will get inside. I’d better close the door.” But Raja told him, “You’re drinking alcohol, you’re smoking a cigarette, and you’re worried about a little smoke that only kills mosquitoes? I want the cool air and to hell with the smoke!” Muthu shrugged and sat back down and they watched the scooter with the fog machine go past. They would be dead within a few hours.

Vijay, his wife Shanthi, and their nine-year-old daughter were just returning home on his motorbike after doing some shopping for vegetables. His daughter was seated just behind him and his wife was behind their daughter and holding onto her. As they were nearing their house the scooter with the fog machine going full blast went past them and Vijay cursed, “Damn it!” He told his wife and daughter as he increased his speed, “Both of you try and cover your nose and mouth, we’ll be home in a minute!" His wife covered her daughter's face with one end of her shawl and covered her own face with the other end. They reached their home and as Vijay parked his bike he told them, "Both of you get into the house and close the door. I'll bring in the vegetables." But by the time he got into the house he had already inhaled a lot of the deadly fumes and had also swallowed some of the particles and he died that night. His wife and daughter had some health issues but survived thanks to his quick thinking of getting them to cover their faces immediately.

Peter Jackson and his wife Janet had built their house in Shanthi Nagar when it had just been opened up as a residential colony and the land was cheap. They had lived there now for the past twenty years and the value of their housing plot had skyrocketed over the last five years. Their daughter was in Chennai studying in college and she lived in the college hostel. Their son lived with them and he had just started working. That evening he was out as usual visiting with his friends and Peter and his wife were sitting in their front yard and enjoying the slight cool breeze of the evening.

When they heard the noise of the fogging machine approaching, his wife got up and said, "Let's go indoors, Peter. That smoke is not good for your asthma." Peter protested and told her, "Come on

Janet, that smoke only kills mosquitoes. This is the only time in the day when we can get some cool natural breeze, and besides, the breeze will blow the smoke away in no time." But Janet was adamant and said, "Don't be lazy, Peter! You can always come out again after the smoke goes away!" Peter sighed and got up as he knew from experience that when his wife was adamant about something there was no point in arguing with her. They went inside and Janet closed the door and then went and locked the windows. She had just finished when she heard the fog machine pass the house. They would later realise that Janet's concern over her husband's asthma had saved them.

Towards the end of the residential colony there was an open space that was earmarked by the corporation to be developed as a playground. But even now the children of the colony would go there in the evenings to play. The boys would kick around a ball while the girls would play throw ball or hopscotch or just walk around the area and talk. There were two streetlights near the open plot and so it was always well lit in the night. When they heard the sound of the fog machine approaching, some of the girls decided to go home since their houses were nearby. Gauri and Girija were sisters and Gauri told her sister, "Let's go home. Mother always says not to inhale this smoke." But Girija was stubborn and said, “I’m just about to win this game. I’ll be careful and not inhale the smoke. Besides, there’s a nice breeze and the smoke will blow away. You go and I’ll come later.” Gauri shrugged and walked away fast to get home before the fog machine passed. So one sister lived and one sister died.

The others stayed and hoped that the smoke would disperse quickly over the open ground. When the fog machine passed the ground there were seven boys and eight girls still there. Over the next thirty days, except for one girl, all the rest would be dead. The girl who survived was twelve years old and she had been wearing a kurta with a shawl. She had covered her face completely with the shawl until the last of the fog had dispersed and so she survived, but not without some serious health issues.

Many of the residents went into their homes as soon as they heard the sound of the fog machine but some stayed outside. There were others who were walking or sitting on the terraces of their houses when the fog machine passed by and they stayed there. Usually, the fog for the mosquitoes would mostly disperse before it reached the terrace of a house, but this time was different. Because the Man had placed the machine at an angle of more than 45 degrees the fog reached the terraces very quickly before dispersing. Most of the people who were on their terraces would be dead within two to four weeks and the rest would have health issues for the remainder of their lives.

The residents of Shanthi Nagar, for the rest of their lives, would always remember this night as the night when silent terror struck!

EXECUTION

MAY 18, TUESDAY - EVENING AND NIGHT

THE MAN

HE REACHED Shanthi Nagar without incident and entered the colony from the street that was the furthest downwind. He drove at a steady, slow speed just as he had practised on this route before. He went down the street and then turned onto the next street and drove down that. He traversed all the streets in the same way, always moving towards the wind so that he would not come in contact with the deadly particles being spewed out of the fog machine strapped to the back of his scooter. He had a scary moment in the middle of his route when he found two cars blocking his way. Both were going in opposite directions and the drivers had stopped and were talking to each other. He frantically signalled to the driver facing him to reverse the car so that he could pass. The smoke was starting to build up around him and, in desperation, he started moving his scooter forward. The driver of the car frowned, but seeing that the Man was determined to pass, he reversed his car and the scooter slipped through. Both drivers caught a full dose of the gas before they could close the windows of their cars.

The Man finally exited the last street and stopped on the main road to switch off the fog machine. He looked at his watch and saw that he had taken more than fifteen minutes to complete his route. Then he continued on his way home. No one was around as he slipped through his gate. He shut the gate and then drove his scooter to the shed. There he carefully removed the machine and the clamps that held it in place from his scooter and dumped everything into the pit at the back of the shed together with all the other containers. Then he removed the black plastic sheets covering the scooter panels and also the fake licence plates. These he also threw into the pit together with his mask and gloves. He removed the khaki clothing and that also went into the pit. In his singlet and shorts he emptied the sacks of mud over the evidence and then covered the pit with the slab and pulled the drum over the slab. But before covering the pit with the slab, he spent some time arranging his little surprise. Then he rearranged all the tyres, tubes, fans, and pipes in a haphazard manner and stood back and looked at the result. He was satisfied that no one would find the pit. But he told himself that if someone did find the pit, then it would be a very bad day for them indeed!

He went into the house and came back with a bucket full of water, some soap, and a big piece of cloth. He carefully cleaned his scooter to get rid of the gum that he had used to stick on the black plastic pieces. Then he fitted his original licence plates back and he was satisfied that no evidence remained that his scooter was used this evening. Finally, he went back inside, bathed and dressed, and waited for the police to come. The time was 8.15 p.m.

MAY 18, TUESDAY - LATE EVENING

THE POLICE

IT WAS NEARLY 7.30 p.m. before Inspector Jamal got back to questioning Faisal. He had been busy going through the findings, or rather the lack of them, from the homes of Faisal and Hariharan as well as their bank accounts and social media accounts. He had discussed everything with the heads of the two teams and he was feeling frustrated. He had ensured that both Faisal and Hariharan were given food and had access to a toilet until he saw them again. He wanted to talk to both the stubborn men only when he had something concrete that he could face them with, but according to the leaders of both teams there was nothing. The Inspector who had led the team to Hariharan's place said, "This guy doesn't even lock his wall closet and there is a locker there that has money and his land deed and other documents!" Jamal asked him, "There was nothing incriminating in any of the documents?" The Inspector shrugged and said, "Unless a certificate of excellence from a renowned college in London is incriminating!" Jamal asked the other Inspector who had gone to Faisal's house, "Don't tell me even Faisal leaves everything open in his house!" The Inspector said, "There was a small wall cupboard that was locked but we opened it without causing any damage."

Jamal sat forward and eagerly asked him, "And what did you find?" The Inspector struggled to keep a smile off his face as he said, "Nothing! This guy is quite a character if you ask me. The small space was empty except for a large piece of paper covered in writing." Jamal impatiently asked him, "Well? Go on, what was written on it? Some literature?" Keeping a straight face, the Inspector told him, "I took a photograph of the message on my phone." He handed his phone to Jamal, who eagerly read the message. The message read, 'I am a Muslim and a social activist and I know that at some point in time the police will raid my place on some excuse. So that they won't be too disappointed at not finding anything, I am keeping this small cupboard locked. Now that you have had the pleasure of raiding my home and opening this cupboard, kindly replace everything and leave my house!'

For a moment, Jamal's face was livid with anger and then he burst out laughing. Shaking his head, he said, "Oh yes! This guy is quite a character and so is the other one I'm afraid." He thought for a moment and then said, "Okay, I'll talk to them and then release them. We have other names on the list, don't we?" One of the inspectors said, "Yes, Sir! There is Swarna, who is an environmentalist, Rajesh, who is a political activist, and then Siva and Prakash, who are both writers by the way." Jamal thought for a moment and then said, "It's late now, past 7 o'clock, and we cannot bring in a lady once it's dark, so it will have to be Rajesh and Siva. Two teams again, one to each house and bring them in for questioning. We'll get to the last guy and the lady tomorrow morning."

He went first to Faisal and said, "You're free to leave and I apologise for the inconvenience. But this is a terrible thing that has happened and we have to question everyone." Faisal stood up and told him, "You're a member of a central investigating team and yet you didn't bother to check if I was even in town at the time of this act of terror. For your information, I was in Chennai for ten days and came back only on the day after this happened." Jamal just said, "We know that you were in Chennai."

Faisal stared at him for a long moment and then said, "Of course! I must have an accomplice!" He walked out of the police station without saying anything else.

When Jamal went to see Hariharan he found him asleep, sitting in a chair with his head resting on his forearm on the table in front of him. He tapped him on the shoulder and Hariharan immediately raised his head. He rubbed his eyes and looked at Jamal and said, "Ah! The secret police returns! What next, truncheons and chains maybe?" Jamal gave him a blank look and said stolidly, "You're free to go and I apologise for the inconvenience. This has been a terrible tragedy and we have to question everyone." Hariharan got up and stretched himself to relieve his cramped muscles. He told Jamal, "I just hope that your people haven't damaged anything in my home or I swear to you that I will file a case for damages against your department!" Jamal simply said, "Nothing has been damaged and you're free to go." Hariharan gave him a long stare but then just shook his head and left without saying anything further.

MAY 18, TUESDAY - NIGHT

THE POLICE

THE TWO TEAMS were dispatched to bring in Rajesh and Siva for questioning. Rajesh wasn't at home when the team reached there and so the Inspector phoned him and told him that he needed to come with them as they wanted to ask him some questions. "We are at your house," the Inspector told him. "You need to come back right now or if you tell us where you are then we can pick you up." Rajesh seemed unworried and he said, "I'll do one better. I'm pretty close to your police station, so I'll leave right now and go there." The Inspector phoned Jamal and told him that Rajesh would be coming in on his own. "He says he is nearby to the station," said the Inspector. "So he will reach the station before we do." Jamal told him, "Don't worry, I'll meet him when he comes in; you search the house."

The second team, which was headed by Inspector Vishal, went to Siva's house and rang the front doorbell on the ground floor. Siva's mother opened the door and stared at the uniforms. "Why do the police always want to talk to my son?" she asked Inspector Vishal. "The other day two people came and spoke to him for a long time and now here you are again! There is nothing that my son can tell you that will be helpful." Inspector Vishal started to say something but she cut him off. "When he wrote his book about such a calamity happening no one listened to him. What were you people doing then? You should have listened to him at that time and maybe this calamity would not have happened. What is the use of asking him things now?" Inspector Vishal held up his hand and said in a firm voice, "Madam! We need to take your son to the police station for questioning. Where is he?" She was shocked and exclaimed, "What do you mean for questioning? He has not done anything wrong! He's a very good boy! You should be ashamed of yourself! Instead of catching the terrorist who did this terrible thing you are harassing an innocent boy!"

Inspector Vishal said with exasperation, "Enough! Madam, if you do not answer me then I will have to take you to the police station as well. Now where is Siva?" She gave him a sullen look and muttered, "He lives on the top floor." Then she shut the door in his face. Inspector Vishal stared at the door for a moment, but then shaking his head he led the way up the stairs. As soon as he knocked on the door it opened and Siva came out. "My mother just phoned and said that you need me for questioning," he said. "I'm ready, so let's go!" Inspector Vishal suppressed the surprise that he felt and instead said formally, "We are here to take you in for questioning. You are not being arrested at the moment as we just wish to question you." Siva frowned and then exclaimed, "I get it, I get it! So let's go now!" Inspector Vishal thought to himself that this mother and son were indeed very interesting people. He took Siva to the police station and placed him in a room. "Inspector Jamal will be with you shortly," he told him. The time was almost 8.45 p.m.

Inspector Jamal first went and spoke to Rajesh as he had arrived just before Siva. He asked Rajesh, "You had stated in an interview with a television channel after the Dalit village incident that such a thing might take place on a larger scale just to embarrass the government. What prompted you to make that statement?" Rajesh said, "I'm a political analyst and I always think of such things. If some nut wanted to embarrass the government then he could do the same thing on a larger scale, just like what has happened now." He paused and then said, "Of course, I was talking about contamination of the water supply to spark a mass outbreak of dysentery or diarrhoea or something along those lines. I never thought that someone would actually *poison* the water supply." Jamal told him, "But it works just as well, doesn't it? In fact, something like this can be the greatest embarrassment for the government and can even bring down a government!" Rajesh scratched his head and said, "I suppose so, but this seems like the act of a terrorist or some nutcase and not some political activist with extreme views. I don't think any political person in this country would go to such lengths to bring down the government."

Jamal said sharply, "But someone like you could!" Rajesh suddenly sat up straight and exclaimed, "Are you saying that you are accusing me of poisoning the water? Just because I made what is a logical statement on television? You can't be serious!" Jamal looked at him stolidly and said, "You are a political activist but you are a supporter of the opposition party and not the ruling party." Rajesh was livid and he shouted, "Are you out of your mind! Do you just pick up people and accuse them of something like this without any rhyme or reason?" Jamal said stolidly, "There is no need to get agitated. I am not accusing you, I am just asking questions."

Rajesh sighed and calmed down. He told Jamal, "This is crazy and I am not going to let you browbeat me or get me to say something that you can later twist to suit your own agenda. Arrest me if you want, but I am not saying another word until I speak with my lawyer." He remained silent after that, although Jamal hammered him with questions for a long time. Finally, Jamal told him, "If you need anything to eat or drink or if you need to use the toilet just knock on the door and a policeman will help you. I will speak to you again later."

It was almost 9 p.m. by the time Jamal sat down to speak to Siva. "You wrote a book about such a thing happening and it wasn't well received," he told him. "Did that make you frustrated and angry?" Siva said heatedly, "Of course it did! Such stupid people in the world nowadays! It was a well-thought-out book and yet people said that such things will not happen. Well, it did happen, didn't it? The trouble is that stupid people will only listen after the event and not before!" Jamal raised his voice and told him, "So you decided to make it happen! When did you first think that you should do something like this to vindicate your book?" Siva looked confused for a moment but then he gave Jamal a sly look and asked him, "So you think that I poisoned the water?"

Jamal told him, "You wrote about it and people disparaged your ideas. You grew angry and frustrated, so it's logical that the next step would be to make your book a reality to prove to people just how clever you are." Siva still had a sly look on his face as he asked him, "So you believe that only a really clever and capable person could do something like that?" Jamal replied, "Yes, only an intelligent person would be able to carry out something dangerous like that." Siva sat up straight and said, "You are right! I did it and now those people who ridiculed me will have to eat their words!"

Jamal stared at him for a long moment and then said, "So you admit that you poisoned the water." Siva nodded and exclaimed, "Yes, I did it!" Jamal asked him, "Tell me, how did you manage to procure the poison?" Siva suddenly looked confused, but then said evasively, "Oh, that wasn't so hard, you know! But I will not tell you all my secrets; maybe later, but not right now." Jamal drummed his fingers on the tabletop and then stood up. "You wait here," he told him. "I'll be in again later to talk to you some more."

He went out and found the police station in chaos. Inspector Gopal was shouting out to a policeman, "Phone Sub-Inspector Ramya and tell her to come here immediately! If she is with David Joseph then tell her to bring him here also." Superintendent of Police Raj Kumar was on the phone and he seemed to be talking to the city police headquarters. Inspector Hari was telling the head constable, "Give everyone masks and gloves and let's move fast!" Jamal went up to Raj and asked him, "What the hell is happening now?" Raj told him, "There's been another attack of some kind. We are getting reports that people in Shanthi Nagar are complaining of stomach pain, shivering, severe headaches, and a lot of them are saying that they have difficulty in breathing!" The time was 9.15 p.m.

ANALYSIS

MAY 18, TUESDAY - NIGHT

DAVID AND RAMYA

IT WAS ALMOST 8 p.m. but David and Ramya were still going through and analysing the recorded conversations. Ramya was saying, "So Siva would actually carry out something like this just to prove to the world and therefore to his mother that he was smart and intelligent?" David said, "The underlying motive would simply be to get out from under his mother's thumb. He could then tell her that if he was fully capable of planning and carrying out such a dangerous mission then he did not need her to look after him. He could then tell her that now *she* needed to listen to *him*!" Ramya sighed and said, "But do you think someone like that would actually do something like this, or would it just remain a thought in their mind?" David pondered and then said, "If a person is pushed too far then the thought can easily turn into action. This man is obsessed with trying to prove to his mother that he is smart and capable, but at the same time the years of being subdued by his mother are hard to shake off. Sometimes it doesn't happen and just remains a thought, but if there is a trigger then a person like that could commit mass murder. You see, in his mind he wouldn't be committing mass murder, he would just be achieving his goal of being free of his mother. *That* is the working of an insane mind!"

Ramya said, "But then, wouldn't he just think of killing his mother? So much simpler and yet he is permanently free of her." David agreed but told her, "I'm sure that he has thought of it. But that's the catch! He doesn't really want his mother dead; he doesn't want to be permanently free of her. I'm sure he doesn't realise it himself, but what he really wants is for their roles to be reversed! He wants to subdue her and order her about just like she has controlled him and his father all these years. He wants her to say that she has to listen to him because he's so smart and capable. *That's* the catch!" Ramya asked him, "You think she controls her husband as well?" David shrugged and said, "I would bet on it. If the father was more assertive, then the mother cannot have such control over the son. She could still have control but not to such an extent, because a child will always instinctively go to the other parent for support. A situation like Siva's usually arises only when there is just one person who has total control or dominance."

Ramya remarked, "So you think he is the person." But David was thoughtful when he replied and said, "He could very well be, but there is something else that's not quite right. It's something that struck me at the time as being odd or out of place. In fact, I am sure that there were two things that struck me as odd, but then I got distracted by something else and it slipped my mind. But it's at the back of my mind and I just cannot get at it for now." He thought for a while but then shook his head and said, "Let's finish this first, and with my mind distracted, hopefully I'll remember."

Ramya said, "There's only Prakash left. I'll play the recording." She played the recording and they listened to it. David said, "This man is definitely obsessed, there is no doubt about it. His obsession is as bad, or rather, worse than Siva's!" Ramya was curious and asked him, "Why do you say that it is worse than Siva's obsession?" David told her, "Siva's obsession is about his mother and what he can do to change their roles towards each other. But Prakash is obsessed with himself and his intellect!" Ramya was thoughtful when she remarked, "But he did say that he knew the difficulties that a writer faced and he accepted them. He said that rejections were a part of the life of an author." But David told her, "You are automatically transcribing these conversations, so read that part and then read what he said after that."

Ramya read the transcript and then said, "I see what you mean. Here, I'll read this out. You were talking about rejection and about the value of his book, and this is how he reacted. He said, 'You can recognise that, but did the others? Oh no! They think they are the smart ones, just because they can turn down your work! I tried to explain to so many people what the purpose of the book was, but did they listen? Hah!!' Then again when you remarked that the police thought that this was the work of a madman and not a terrorist, he said, 'They never listen! So many smart people have warned about similar dangers but they never listen! Even now they are not listening I can tell you!' He was very angry when he said those things." She kept staring at the transcript and thinking and then suddenly she looked up at David and said, "I was picturing that conversation in my mind just now as I was reading the transcript and I realised something. You were leading him on! You were...what's the word...*stoking* his ego, or is it stroking...whatever, you were definitely pushing him to see his reactions!"

David smiled in satisfaction and said, “I’m glad you caught that, because I was wondering if you had missed what I was doing. I suspected that there was a smouldering fire within him about his rejections and so I supplied the fuel to see if it would ignite and it did.” Ramya was thoughtful when she remarked, “So both Siva and Prakash are obsessed. Siva is obsessed about his mother and Prakash is obsessed about his rejections.” Suddenly David’s eyes lit up and he said, “Wait, wait! What you just said...his rejections...” Ramya started to speak but David held up his hand for silence while he thought. He was rubbing his chin and frowning for a while and then he looked up at her and said, “Go through that transcript again. Come to the point where I asked him about the purpose of his book. I think it was just after I spoke about the value of his writing and the rejections. That’s the part you first read out. Just after that I think.”

Ramya looked at the transcript and then said, “Yes, when he said that about the purpose of his book, you asked him what the purpose was and he said, ‘To point out the dangers that exist right in front of us! The police are always looking for bombs and guns and what not, but then there is something like this that is staring them in the face and yet they just cannot see it!’ Then you spoke about the police thinking that this was the work of a madman...” But

David cut her off and exclaimed, “That’s it! That’s one of the things that struck me as odd! You see, he was always going on about people not listening and then about the rejection of his book, etc. etc., and so I thought that he was obsessed about his work and himself per se, and therefore he resented the rejection because of that.”

Ramya looked confused and said, “But he *is* obsessed about himself and how clever he is. He kept talking about how this calamity could have been avoided if only people had listened to him and not just rejected his book.” But David smacked his forehead and said, “No! I’m a fool! Read that again and you’ll see. He says the purpose of the book was to point out the *dangers* that exist in front of us! If you go back to the television debate, I’m sure he said something about him writing the article and the book because he was concerned about the lack of *security* around our water supply. During our conversation which you just read out, he told me that his book was more realistic than Siva’s because he wrote about poison being dumped in an overhead tank that supplied water to many areas. That’s *exactly* what happened! He is not so obsessed about himself as he is obsessed about his idea of the lack of security. The more people did not listen, the more they rejected and ridiculed his idea, the more he became obsessed with it!”

Ramya's face was animated as she listened to David and now she said, "So he finally made his book come true!" But David was cautious and he said, "Yes, if that obsession finally drove him beyond the point of sanity and into the darkness of insanity. But there is one more thing that struck me as odd, and if I can recall that then I will be absolutely sure that he is our man. One more thing..."

Just then Ramya's phone rang and she stood up as she listened and David noted the change in her facial expression. She was animated and excited before the phone rang, but her expression now was one of horror! She finished the call by saying, "Yes, I'll be there immediately. Five minutes. Yes, I'll bring him, he is with me." She ended the call and told David, "There has been another attack! In Shanthi Nagar this time! That's about five kilometres from here. Inspector Gopal wants both of us to come to the station right now." David immediately got up and they both raced out of the house and got into the car.

As Ramya drove away at high speed, David phoned Raj. "Yes Raj," he said. "I heard, and Ramya and I are on the way right now, but listen! What are you hearing, what are the symptoms this time?" Raj said, "It seems from the phone calls that came into the station that some people are dead and many are complaining about stomach pain, severe headaches, shivering, and difficulty breathing. It doesn't sound like arsenic poisoning this time and..." David was impatient and cut him off by saying, "Concentrate Raj! Did the reports say when this happened? Did anyone mention any incident just prior to people feeling these symptoms?"

Raj spoke to someone in the station and then told David, "It seems that a corporation mosquito fog machine passed through the area just after dark and before people started falling sick. Two people who phoned in thought that maybe there was something in the mosquito fog that was sprayed in the area, but we are going there right now and..." But again David cut him off and almost shouted, "Raj! Listen to me carefully! This is also arsenic but more dangerous. Anyone going into that area should be fully covered from head to toe. Gather up all the PPE kits available, since I'm sure there are many still in stock, especially at hospitals, after the pandemic. This could be arsine gas, I've been reading about it since this started. It's in the air and most probably the fog machine was used to disperse it."

Raj again started to say something but David cut him off saying, "Please just listen Raj. We don't have much time. You have to check the wind direction and start treating people at least six to seven kilometres downwind. Contact the disaster management authorities right now and explain the situation and let them take charge. Once they know it is a poisonous gas they will take the necessary measures. For now you just make sure that no cop, no doctor, no one goes into that area without a full PPE kit. We'll be in the station in five minutes." Ramya asked David, "Why were you looking up poisonous gases?" David told her, "Because of Siva's book. The ending, remember?" Ramya exclaimed, "Of course! But he wrote about drones!" David agreed but said, "Yes, so I searched the internet to see if it could be done without using drones. While I couldn't find any specific examples, what I did find made me uneasy, because it seemed that it wouldn't be that difficult to disperse this gas. But I never thought of a fog machine!"

MAY 18, TUESDAY - NIGHT

SILENT TERROR

AFTER SPEAKING WITH DAVID, Raj told Inspector Gopal and Inspector Jamal what he had said. "I will contact the disaster management authorities and inform them right now," he said. "You take charge of getting enough PPE kits so we can go to the disaster zone and get people out of there." Gopal did not answer because he was already telling his head constable, "Send men to all the local hospitals and surgical equipment shops and tell them to grab every available PPE full kit. That means the entire kit, remember! The full gown and mask and gloves, everything! As they get some kits they are to rush them immediately here and then go back for more. This is urgent because we cannot do anything unless we have the kits. As soon as the kits start to arrive, suit up as many constables as you can and send them with vans to the area to transport the people to the hospitals. Commandeer a bus or two and use that as well."

He turned to Raj and said, "We have about five full kits right here in the station that we can use. I am going over there right now so are you coming with me?" Just then David and Ramya ran into the station and they heard what Gopal was saying. Ramya immediately said, "Sir, I'm coming with you!" David also said, "Count me in!" Raj told Gopal, "You said five kits, didn't you? There's you, Ramya, David, Hari, and I, so that makes five. Let's move!" Inspector Jamal said, "David, I need to speak to you." But David was leaving the room with the others and he said over his shoulder, "Not now Inspector. I must go to the affected area and see if I am right, otherwise we will have to change the information we gave to the disaster management authorities!"

He told Gopal, "Have police vans waiting just upwind of the area and we can send the people to them. For now, have your people inform the hospitals that these victims should be kept in isolation and treated for arsine gas inhalation. If I am wrong then we can correct them later. And another thing that I remember reading, tell the hospitals no chelation therapy!" Raj said, "I have the number of that doctor we met the first time who helped us in writing out the treatment protocols. I'll call him now." He phoned the doctor and handed over the phone to David. After David had told the doctor what to expect, he asked him to write out the instructions and told him that a policeman would pick it up and get it distributed to the other hospitals and clinics. He told Gopal, "Send a man to that doctor to get the instructions and then get it circulated to all the clinics and hospitals."

All five of them got fully suited up and they left in a police van because they wouldn't have fitted in a car dressed as they were in the full PPE kits. It took them almost ten minutes to reach Shanthi Nagar due to the late evening traffic. When they got there David told the others, "Let's split up and talk to as many people as we can. The first thing is to get the people moving upwind and out of this area. Find out if people remember when the fog machine passed them and how long after that did they develop any symptoms. Make a note of all the symptoms that people say they are experiencing. Also ask them if anything else unusual happened this afternoon or evening." Gopal said, "I've told the Writer to contact the corporation and find out if they had any fogging planned for this area today." David replied, "That's good, but that's for later. Right now we need to find out if I have made the right call!"

They split up and each of them took a different

street and went house by house. The first thing that struck Ramya was the difference between this disaster zone and the previous one. When she had gone to Ram Nagar she saw chaos; people were screaming, there were people vomiting in the street, she saw people curled up on the street moaning in pain, and she saw a lot of dead bodies. Here there was no screaming, just an eerie silence. There were people standing and talking or walking about the street aimlessly. Some were sitting by their front doors holding their heads in their hands. Almost everyone she saw looked worried but she sensed the heavy palpable fear that hung over everyone. She realised that the eerie silence was because people, almost unknowingly, were talking in whispers.

She walked up to the nearest group of people that were standing on the road and talking amongst themselves. They stared at her as she approached and she saw first their look of surprise and then she saw that surprise turn to fear as they looked at her in the full PPE suit. One man asked her in a panic-stricken voice, "What is happening? Is this another pandemic attack? Why weren't we informed that something like this would happen?" She told them in a calm voice, "This is not a pandemic. I am with the police and we are here to help you. Are any of you experiencing symptoms like headache, stomach pain, shivering, or difficulty breathing?" Another man said, “Many are having difficulty breathing but we thought that it was something in the mosquito fog that was sprayed here this evening. I noticed that this time it seemed to have a different sort of smell. Some people were having stomach pain and vomiting and they have mostly gone to the hospital. Others are complaining of severe headaches. We have been talking about what we should do.”

The first man said, “We phoned the police and they just told us to wait here, that they would send someone.” Ramya asked him, “Do you remember when the fog machine passed through this area?” The man said, “Just after darkness fell, so it would have been after 7 p.m.” Ramya then asked him, “And how long after that did people start complaining of these symptoms?” The men looked at one another and then one man said, “It would have been about an hour or so, maybe 8 or 8.30 p.m. I phoned the police at 9 o’clock when I realised that people from almost all the streets in the area were complaining of these symptoms. Are you saying that the fog smoke is responsible for this? Some sort of contamination?”

Ramya told them, “I want you to round up as many people as you can and all of you go down the road at the end of this colony. You see the way the wind is blowing? Walk down the road towards the wind, always have the wind in your face, and you will find police vans waiting there to take you to the hospitals. Please spread the word to everyone. It is important that you evacuate this area as soon as possible." When they all tried to ask her questions at the same time she said, "The police will issue a press release shortly, but until then please do as I have instructed. It is for your own safety."

She moved on, but not before she saw them run straight down the road for the police vans. Only two men stayed and started going house to house shouting out to the residents to come out and evacuate the area. When she came to the next street she saw that most of the houses were empty, but four houses down the line she came to a stop when she saw a small house with the front door thrown wide open. She walked up to the door and saw two men sitting in chairs with their heads on the table between them. They seemed to be sleeping and she went in and checked them, but found that they were dead. Slowly she moved out of the house and stood in the street. She stood there just staring at the ground. She was vaguely aware that she should move on but her mind refused to function and she just stood there.

David went to the first gate on his left and he shouted out, "If anyone is in there please come out. We are with the police and we are here to help you." The house happened to be Fatima's and she opened the front window just a crack and shouted through it, "I'm not coming out! My friends have phoned and told me that people are dying and falling sick! I'm sure it was that mosquito fogging that went by about three hours ago." As she was speaking, David opened the gate and walked up to the window. He asked her, "Madam can you tell me if you are experiencing any stomach pain or headache? Are you shivering or feeling like vomiting?" She told him, "We are all fine here. I always shut my doors and windows when that fogging starts and after the phone calls I just didn't open anything. What is happening?" David asked her, "Are you feeling any type of symptoms at all?" She spoke to someone in the house and then told him, "No, we are all quite normal. What should we do now?"

David thought for a moment and then told her, "Just stay there and keep everything locked for at least another two hours. By that time the disaster management team will be here and they will tell you what to do." She told him, "Please see if my neighbour is okay. That house just across the street from mine."

David walked over to the house and shouted at the window, "If anyone is in there just open this window a little. Do not open it fully!" The window cracked open just a sliver and a male voice said, "Who are you and what is happening out there? We got phone calls that people were dying and could not breathe." David told him, "Are you experiencing any symptoms like stomach pain, headache, shivering, difficulty breathing, or any itching of the skin?" The man replied, "Nothing, we closed everything when the fog machine passed thanks to our neighbour Fatima across the road. People are saying that the fogging is responsible for all this." David told him, "Just stay there with everything locked for the next two hours until the disaster management team gets here and then they will take over."

He went down to the next house and found the door open. A man came to the door when he called out. David asked him, "Are you having any symptoms? Difficulty breathing, headaches?" The man said with difficulty, "I can hardly breathe and my wife is having a terrible headache. My son says his stomach is paining. What the hell is happening?" David told him, "If you can take your family to the end of this colony, just down the road you will find police vans and they will take you to the hospital. You see the direction that the wind is blowing? Go down the road facing the wind and you will find the police vans. Please go immediately." A boy who looked to be around sixteen or seventeen years old came to the door and said, "I'll take my parents on my father's bike right now." David asked them, "Do you remember when the fog machine passed this way?" The man said, "Just after darkness fell, so it must have been around 7 or 7.15. Why?"

David ignored the question and asked him, "And how long after that did you start experiencing these symptoms?" The man said, "Why are you asking me these questions? Was the mosquito fogging contaminated?" David said, "Please Sir, this is important and there is no time to waste. Everything will be explained as soon as the disaster management team gets here." The young boy came in front of his father and said, "My father started having difficulty with breathing about 8.00 p.m. and my mother and I started feeling bad about an hour later." David asked him, "Where was your father when the fog machine passed by?" The boy replied, "He was sitting here by the front door for the cool air. My mother was in the kitchen and I was in my bedroom studying."

David thanked him and said, "All of you get to those police vans and they will take you to the hospital." The boy asked him, "Sir! Does it mean that everyone has to go to the hospital?" David said, "Yes, I'm afraid so." The boy told him, "You would take too long to walk the streets telling people. I will drop my parents at the van and I will go around on my bike and tell people to go to the police vans." David stopped and stared at him, "I'm an idiot," he said. "You take your parents to the van and you also go to the hospital. I will take care of this. Thank you!"

He took out his phone with difficulty and called Raj. He told him, "Get a police van to run through these streets with a loudspeaker telling everyone where the police vans will be. They are to tell them to go immediately there and be taken to the hospital. Do it now Raj because I'm sure this is arsine gas poisoning or some variant of it at least!"

By the time the police van came and went around making the loudspeaker announcement, David had traversed the street and was on the second street where he met Ramya. She was just standing and staring at the ground and he rushed up to her. When he reached her he saw that she was standing in front of a small house. She looked at him and then just pointed at the house. The front door stood wide open and David saw the two men sitting in chairs with their heads resting on the table. He made to go inside but Ramya held him back and said, "I checked. They're dead." David looked at her and realised that just a few days back she had seen the horrors of the arsenic poisoning of the water and now this! He gently pushed her towards the road and said, "There is no need for us to be here any longer. I've found out all that I need to know. Let's go back to the station." He took out his phone and called Raj and told him to meet them at the van. All five met at the police van that they had come in and they went back to the police station.

The people of the area meanwhile had started to make their way to the police vans from where they were taken to the hospitals and clinics in the vans and in the buses. Two police vans with two constables in each van dressed in full PPE kit went around the area, and when they found people who could not walk to the road, they piled them into the vans and took them to the end of the road and loaded them into the buses that the police had commandeered. Then they came back and started going around the area again. They did this until no one was left in the area, including Fatima and her family and her neighbour. The disaster management team were on their way but they had phoned ahead and told the police what information they were to give to all the hospitals and clinics where the people were being taken. Since they had been told by Raj that it was an arsine gas attack or something similar they gave instructions for treatment based on that. Their instructions weren't that different from what David and the local doctor had already distributed.

MAY 18, TUESDAY - NIGHT

PROFILING

DAVID and the others had removed their PPE suits and were sitting in Gopal's office, having some coffee when Inspector Jamal barged in and said, "David, I told you that I needed to speak to you!"

David said mildly, "We've just returned. You're here now so go ahead and tell me."

Jamal said, "This could have been avoided if only you had shared your thoughts with us from the beginning!"

David still spoke mildly and asked him, "And how would it have been avoided?"

Jamal said with a slight note of triumph in his voice, "Because we have arrested the criminal! And if you had shared your thoughts with us from the beginning, we would have arrested him sooner and this attack would not have taken place."

Raj jumped up and exclaimed, "You have arrested him? That's damn good work, Inspector! Who is he?"

Jamal said with almost a smirk, "The writer, Siva! We picked him up for questioning around 8.30 p.m., so he must have just completed this attack and gone home before we picked him up."

They all looked at David, who was rubbing his chin thoughtfully. Raj asked him, "David? Did you suspect Siva?"

David looked up at him and said, "We suspected everyone and Siva was a prime candidate." He looked at Inspector Jamal and said, "But he is not the person who committed these acts. You have the wrong man."

Inspector Jamal took a deep breath and then told him, "I know about your reputation, but in this case, you are wrong! And do you know why you are wrong?" He didn't wait for an answer but continued, "Because Siva has confessed!"

Raj intervened and told Inspector Jamal, "Maybe you should listen to what David has to say before you go ahead with arresting Siva. At least listen to his reasoning before you decide."

But Inspector Jamal said, "*You* listen to him and then you decide what you want to do. After all, you're from a different department altogether, so you go ahead on your own without me. I know what

I'm doing and I have a confession, so I'm done with listening now."

David sighed and told Inspector Jamal, "I knew that telling you my angle on this case would be a mistake. It was a mistake because I knew that you would go about arresting everyone, and I was afraid that that action would trigger the second attack. Now that has happened! But if you are convinced that you have the man responsible, then so be it. But if you want my opinion, then I must say that you have the wrong man."

Inspector Jamal stared at him for a long moment, then made a derisive sound and walked out of the room.

Ramya asked David, "He confessed? Why would he do that?"

Before David could reply, Raj told him, "David, you need to tell me what's going on. Are you sure Inspector Jamal has the wrong man? Then why would he confess to something if he wasn't guilty?"

David told him, "Siva *is* obsessed, there is no doubt about that, and that obsession has made him insane on that point. Remember I said that if this was the work of an individual, then it could be the work of an insane mind. I made a distinction between what I meant by an insane mind and a person who had gone totally insane. I said that sometimes a person can become so obsessed with something that their mind can go insane on that one fixation, but they will be quite normal otherwise. Of course, eventually they will go totally insane without proper therapy."

Raj's eyes opened wide in surprise, and he said, "Of course! Like that girl who became obsessed with that guy... what was his name... Harish! Yes, I get it now."

Ramya asked Raj, "You had a case like this one before?"

Raj told her, "Well, a person with an obsession like the one David is describing now. This girl, from her schooldays, was in love with a boy named Harish. It was unrequited love, but she refused to accept that fact. Eventually, that love became an obsession, and she managed to blackmail him for some time until he suddenly left his hometown. But when he got married, she got to hear of it, and she followed him. To cut a long, sad story short, she hired men to kill him, and she would have killed his wife as well if not for David unravelling the whole sordid tale. The point is that, if you spoke to her, she was quite normal and sane about everything else."

Ramya asked him, "So what happened to her?"

Raj shrugged and said, "She was declared insane and she is in a mental facility. The last I heard, she had gone completely mad."

He turned to David and said, "Okay, I get it now,

but if Siva also has an insane mind and he is so obsessed, then why do you think that he isn't guilty? Especially after Inspector Jamal says that he has confessed."

So David explained it to him.

"Siva's obsession is about his mother's control over him," he said. "She decides everything for him, and she has made him believe that without her to guide him he cannot achieve anything. I'm pretty sure that the book he wrote on poisoning the waters of a dam was actually her idea. I'm also sure that she got that idea from an article that the journalist Mahesh wrote about the same subject. When the book was trolled and people told Siva that such a thing was a bit farfetched, his mother immediately convinced him that the people were stupid and that his idea was brilliant. You must remember that it was actually her idea in the first place. I think that eventually Siva realised what was happening to him and he now desperately wants to get out from under his mother's control. That's his obsession and that's where his mind is insane. He will gladly confess to this crime because it will be his way of showing his mother that finally he did something independently without his mother's approval or guidance. In his mind, the fact that the attacks were carried out successfully means that he is a success without his mother's help."

He paused in thought for a moment and then said, "I would be willing to bet that Inspector Jamal first accused him of contaminating the water supply and he confessed after that. As I said, he has an insane mind but he is not the guilty person. He is a deeply disturbed young man who is in need of urgent therapy, and I am sure that, given time, he will recover fully."

Raj told him, "I get all that, David, but for a moment just look at it this way. He wants to show his mother what he can do on his own, just like you said, so he goes and poisons the water. Nobody accuses him, so since he succeeded once he then goes and carries out the second attack. Remember, in his book he does talk about an air attack and that too with drones. So he succeeds in his second attack as well. Now when he is picked up and Jamal accuses him, he happily confesses because, like you said, he wants his mother to know that he doesn't need her anymore! Now tell me what's wrong with that argument."

Hari chimed in and said, "He's learnt a lot over the years from you, David! Nowadays he even gives *me* lessons in psychology."

David was serious and he told Raj, "I agree that it is a sound hypothesis, except for one point. His single obsession is that he wants to prove to his mother that he doesn't need her and that he can act independently. So if he did the poisoning of the water tank and since that attack succeeded, then he would have confessed immediately. There was no need for the second attack to achieve what his insane mind demanded because the first attack had already done that. He would have shouted it from the rooftops in exultation because in his mind he would have finally broken his mother's control over him."

Raj started to say something but David held up his hand and said, "Wait Raj, you were also saying that he is responsible because he wrote about the air attack using drones in his book. The article that Mahesh wrote two to three years ago was about the possibility of the dam waters being poisoned with the use of drones. In Siva's book the dam waters are poisoned and the air attack is done with drones. As I said, I am sure that his mother got the idea from Mahesh's article and she put it to her son as though it was her own idea." He paused for a moment and then said, "I can tell you this with absolute certainty. Inspector Jamal is not going to find any evidence to back up Siva's confession."

Hari remarked, "He might, David, if the actual criminal plants some evidence at Siva's house."

But David disagreed and told him, "No Hari, that won't happen, for the simple reason that we're not dealing with an ordinary criminal. We are dealing with an insane mind with one fixed objective, and no way is that person going to give the credit to someone else once he has succeeded in that objective."

Ramya exclaimed, "So it was Prakash!"

David looked at her and said, "Smart girl! Yes, I am sure that it is Prakash. Remember I had told you that there were two things that I had forgotten with all the distractions?"

Ramya said, "Yes, I remember. You had said that he was obsessed with himself, and when I read out the transcript you exclaimed that he was obsessed not with himself but with his idea about the lack of security. You said that that was one of the two things that were pushed to the back of your mind."

David raised his eyebrows and said, "Nothing wrong with *your* memory!" Ramya smiled a little at the praise but then asked him, "So you remembered the second thing?"

David sighed and said, "Actually, I was on the verge of remembering that when you got the phone call for us to come to the station. But yes, I remembered it when you read out the transcript. I had goaded him about the phone call that the others had received from a stranger and finally he pretended to remember it. Wait, it will still be on my phone, so you can play it for us." He gave his phone to Ramya and she found the recording and played it.

They heard Prakash saying, 'No, it was after the interview, and so I thought it was someone who had watched the program. Besides, I just thought that he was comparing both the books. You know, Siva's book and mine.' David said, "There it is! But go to the point where I asked him about the exact words spoken during that phone call and then he pretended to recall what was said. He spoke about his book again."

Ramya fast-forwarded until she came to the point that David was talking about. She played it and raised the volume and they all listened to Prakash saying, 'You were spot on with your book. That was very well written and something like that is bound to happen but ignorant people will never really see what is right in front of their faces! Siva's book was good too, but it can't happen like that and I'm sure the end is wrong where he talks about drones.'

Raj looked sceptical and he said, "Okay, so the caller praised his book and compared it to Siva's and he also disagreed about the use of drones, so what?"

David told him, "The point is that the caller could not have known what was in the book that Prakash wrote, so how could he compare it with Siva's?"

This time Ramya looked surprised and asked him, "Why not? Why couldn't he have known? You said that Prakash wrote about the poisoning of the water tank..." Her voice trailed off and David said, "Exactly! Now you get it."

He told Raj, "The caller couldn't have known because Prakash's book was never published, so how could he compare both the books? And how would he know if Prakash's book was well written or not without being able to read it?"

Raj was now confused and he said, "But you knew..."

This time Ramya interrupted and told David, "I should have seen that! It was right in front of me! No wonder you are *the*..."

She stopped when David gave her a look and Hari laughed and told her, "Don't worry, we all get that look at times. He just hates to be called *the* David Joseph."

But David smiled and told Ramya, "Don't notice him, he takes advantage because he married my elder stepdaughter!"

Ramya looked at David, Raj, and Hari and remarked, "You guys are all related, but what you have is something that goes beyond that and I'm envious. There is a closeness that you three have, and sometimes it appears to others as though you can read each other's minds!"

It was Hari who answered her. "Yes, there's a bond between us, but that bond was forged through murder and horror and shared danger. We've been together and worked together for quite a number of years now. When that psychopath targeted David, it put everyone in danger. But we got through it because we could always depend on each other."

David said mildly, "Let the girl speak."

Ramya sighed and said, "Yes, as I was saying, I should have seen that."

Raj interrupted to say, "As *I* was saying, since *you* knew about what Prakash wrote, then why couldn't the caller have known."

It was Ramya who told him, "We knew because Prakash told us. David had suggested that his book was rejected because Siva had already written a book on the subject and Prakash immediately put down Siva's book as not being quite realistic and told us about his book. He told us that he had actually written about poisoning a large water tank."

Raj said, "But he could have spoken about it elsewhere, like the television interview."

But Ramya again said, "No, we had listened to that footage and the exact story wasn't mentioned. Besides, as David just pointed out, even if the caller had heard about the story, how would he know if the book was well written when he couldn't have read the book!"

Raj said, "So you're saying that he never got a phone call and he just made up what he said."

David told him, "He never got a phone call because he was the one who made the phone calls to others. We have the dates and the timings of those calls, and Ramya has requested for the phone logs so that will give you the evidence you need. I had told him that everyone else got those phone calls and so he didn't want to be the odd man out. I also told him that Siva had remembered the calls perfectly so he pretended to do the same."

Ramya told David, "When I read the transcript, it was obvious to me that you were leading him on. Even that bit where you told him about how to go back and remember the call? That was not the actual method, because that is not the method that you outlined to the others and to me for that matter. So what made you do that?"

Hari told her, "When David has a sixth sense that something is off with a person, then he will try his best to get that person to slip up using devious means. And he has a lot of devious methods up his sleeve, believe me!"

Ramya said, "Well, Prakash certainly fell for it. He even said that he was able to recall the conversation only by doing what David had suggested." She then asked David, "So why did he mention the ending of Siva's book and the drones?"

David said, "That was the one thing that I didn't catch on to. He liked the idea of an air attack, but he considered the use of drones as not feasible. He must have mentioned it only because he had already planned an air attack using the fog machine!"

Raj remarked, "This guy appears to be very intelligent. To pull off these two attacks without being caught takes intelligence. What I can never quite figure out is why people with intelligence would waste that intellect on doing such criminal acts!"

David told him, "Oh, he's definitely intelligent! While others hypothesised about terror attacks using drones to poison the water in our large dams, this man spotted the most vulnerable area that could easily be exploited if our security wasn't tightened up. But nobody listened. Prakash knows that he is intelligent and he must have been proud of himself that he was able to expose such a simple but dangerous gap in our security. It must have eaten into his soul that the authorities just wouldn't pay attention to what he was saying. Over time, such a fixation can become an obsession until finally that obsession creates an insane mind."

Raj said, "That sounds as though you are saying that the authorities are responsible for what this man did."

David sighed and told him, "Yes, they are, although I am not saying that to justify what he did. As I have told you so often, a true psychopath is born and not made. They are born with a lack of the human emotion that we call a conscience, and therefore for them there is no right or wrong. For them there only exists their desires and impulses, and they don't see it as right or wrong. They don't need a trigger to do the terrible things that they do, they do it because they want to do it, because they enjoy doing it! But people like Prakash, or Siva for that matter, are different because they are born with a sane mind and then some trigger turns that mind insane."

He paused to collect his thoughts and then continued. "Take Sarojini for instance. She was born quite normal, but she became obsessed with Harish until that obsession made her insane. What if Harish had loved her in return? Would she then have turned insane or would she have remained normal and lived a happy married life? Or was there something in her genes that would have anyway triggered that effect due to some other obsession that she may have developed later on in life? These are questions that are hard to answer because the human mind is more complex than we can ever imagine. But the point is that Sarojini and Prakash needed a trigger for their minds to become insane, albeit insane only with regard to that one obsession."

Suddenly Hari exclaimed, "While we are sitting here and talking, that man could be getting away or destroying evidence. Shouldn't we move quickly and arrest him before he disappears?"

But David told him, "He won't disappear. He will be sitting in his house waiting for the police to come."

Raj asked him, "Are you saying that he thinks the police are onto him?"

David shook his head and said, "No, but since he knows that Inspector Jamal is picking up all the people that I interviewed, then he knows that they will be coming to pick him up as well. I told you this would happen. Because Inspector Jamal started picking up the people who had spoken of the lack of security with our water supply, that triggered the second attack. To Prakash, it meant that they were still not taking the issue of security seriously and were instead shooting the messenger. So he carried out the second attack." He thought for a moment and then told Ramya, "I think if we go back to that transcript, we will find that he said something similar to us."

Ramya said, "I don't have to. He was very angry that they had picked up Faisal and Hariharan, and he said that it showed that the police were not taking security seriously. I remember at the end he said...wait a minute, I'll play it." She went to the end of the recording and they heard Prakash say, 'Well, let's hope the authorities are taking security seriously. And if they want to come for me next, well, here I am so let them come! I will be ready and willing to answer them.'

Raj said slowly, "So you believe that he will be waiting for us. Do you think that he would have destroyed any evidence?"

David thought for a moment and then said, "He might not have, but if he didn't then he would have hidden it well and you will have to search for it. I think it doesn't matter to him if he is caught, because then that would really throw the spotlight on the authorities not taking the security of our water supply seriously despite Prakash's warnings. But you can be sure that he won't make things too easy for you. The more I think of it, the more I am sure that the evidence will be there but you will have to find it."

Raj told him, "Well, we are going right now to arrest him. You want to come along?"

Ramya immediately said, "I am coming with you!" She turned to David and asked him, "David, you are coming too, aren't you?" But David didn't hear her because he was deep in thought and staring blankly at the opposite wall.

Raj told her softly, "He's thinking, so just wait. He has this capacity to shut out the world and go deep into his mind when he is solving a problem!"

After a while David's eyes came into focus and

he told Ramya, "Yes, we will go along with them and we will take two constables along as well."

Hari said, "I think we are enough to handle this guy, David. It's not as though he's a dreaded terrorist and will be waiting for us with guns and bombs!"

David told him, "No, he won't be waiting with guns and bombs because he has something just as deadly! I remember reading that arsine gas can be produced with the addition of acid. If that is what he has done, then he would have had to modify the fog machine, I think. I'm no expert on fog machines, but I think he would have had to make *some* modifications at least."

Raj exclaimed, "David, this guy is just a writer!"

But Ramya told him, "No, not just a writer! He is an engineer who turned to writing later on in life."

Raj frowned and asked David, "So what are you thinking?"

David said, "I'm not quite sure, but listening to the end of the recording just now where he said that he would be waiting for the police and that he would be ready and willing to answer them...there's something in the way that he said that. It made me wonder if he was planning an explosive end to this sordid tale. Something that would hit the headlines and everyone would then know what he had done, and more importantly, to him, *why* he did it!"

Hari remarked, "So, a booby trap."

David rubbed his chin and said, "Thinking logically, maybe a device that would drop the arsenic into the acid, thereby producing arsine gas. You would be talking to him and telling him that he is under arrest and he could trigger the device."

Hari said, "And since we don't have any idea about what the device might be, there would be no way to stop him."

Raj was frowning in thought and now he asked David, "So why the two constables?"

David told him, "Because I'm thinking that his ego would suggest to him that his arrest would be done only by a top officer of the police. Seeing just two constables could throw him off his stride and lull his suspicions and that is very important if we are to avoid another calamity. Remember, if the gas is triggered, then it will not be just the police and him who are affected. The gas would drift with the wind and many more would be affected as well."

Raj said, "Okay, let's take it for granted that he has a booby trap ready for us. The device would have to be in his house and not outside, because if it was outside then we might not be affected, although a lot of people downwind would be."

Hari told him, "But how can he be sure that we will come inside? We could just ring the bell and arrest him when he opens the door! In that case, the device would have to be outside and not inside the house."

Ramya interrupted and asked David, "Will the device be inside or outside the house, David?"

David told her, "I think that Raj is right and so is Hari."

Ramya frowned and Hari said, "How can we both be right! It must be either inside or outside."

David did not answer him. Suddenly both Ramya and Raj spoke at the same time, "The hiding place!"

David smiled and Hari remarked ruefully, "You can see that she is aiming to be a Superintendent as soon as possible!"

Raj was thinking and now he said, "If it's the hiding place, then I doubt if he would have any kind of remote trigger for the trap, but let's not take any chances. I think most probably it would be mechanical. If we move something then the trap would trigger or something on those lines. So here's what we will do." Everyone agreed with his plan and they made their preparations and left for Prakash's house. The time was 11p.m.

MAY 18, TUESDAY - 11 P.M. TO MIDNIGHT

THE ARREST

THEY REACHED Prakash's house within ten minutes. David, Raj, and Hari had come by car and they parked the car down the street out of sight of his house. Ramya and the two constables had come in a police van and they approached from the opposite side of the street where again they parked the van out of sight of Prakash's house. David and Raj walked down the road with Hari until they reached the property of Prakash's neighbour. David and Raj waited on the road while Hari entered the property. Ramya exited the police van and approached Prakash's house from that side. She walked down the road and entered the compound of Prakash's neighbour. She found the place to be dark and assumed that the people had gone to bed.

There was a common compound wall between

the two properties which was around five feet in height. She cautiously looked over the wall and saw that the windows of Prakash's house on this side were closed. There was only faint moonlight and the area was shrouded in shadows. Taking a deep breath she pulled herself up and swung her body over the wall and landed without a sound on the other side. Walking silently she reached the side of Prakash's house where she waited just around the corner of the front wall and sent a missed call to one of the constables who were waiting in the police van. From the other side Hari carried out the same manoeuvre, and once he was in place at the side of Prakash's house, he sent a missed call to Raj.

As soon as the constable received the missed call he started the van and drove to Prakash's house. The police van rolled to a stop in front of the house and the two constables exited the van and walked up to the front door. They rang the bell and waited for a minute and then rang it again. Suddenly the gate lights and a light above the front door came on and the whole area was bathed in brightness. The front door opened halfway and Prakash looked out at the two tall constables. "What do you want?" he asked them. One of the constables told him, "Sir, we have been asked to bring you down to the station for questioning." Prakash came forward a little and looked all around but he could see no one else. "I would have expected to see at least an Inspector if you've come to pick me up," he told them. "They did send Inspectors to pick up Hariharan and Faisal!"

The constable told him, "That could be because they were suspected of having some involvement in this case. The protocol would then be that only a Sub-Inspector or an Inspector can pick them up." Prakash stared at him for a moment and then asked, "And in my case?" The constable shrugged and told him, "I wouldn't know, Sir. You asked me about the others and I was just stating the usual protocol. In your case we were just told to come and pick you up for questioning." The other constable added, "I heard them saying that you would be able to figure out something, but I don't know what they were talking about."

Prakash opened the door and stepped out onto the porch. He peered suspiciously at the van parked in front of the gate and said, "Maybe the Inspector is waiting in the van." As they had been instructed to do, the two constables moved aside and Prakash stepped off the porch. He was still looking at the van and his peripheral vision was blocked by the tall constables. Silently Hari and Ramya moved swiftly forward, and when the constables sensed that they were near they took a step away from them and Hari and Ramya pounced on Prakash. They each grabbed one of Prakash's hands and they expertly knocked his legs out from under him and he fell flat on his back. Prakash had only a brief second to see the constables take a step away before his hands were held and then he was flat on the ground.

Hari and Ramya then flipped him over and handcuffed him behind his back. Then they stood him up and while the constables held him, Hari searched him deftly and swiftly. Prakash was fully dressed and Hari searched his pockets and patted him down expertly but he found nothing dangerous. He whistled, and in a minute Raj and David walked through the front gate. Prakash gave them a grim smile and told David, "So you are one of them. I thought that you really understood what I had said." David told him, "Oh, yes! I really did understand and that's why we are here. By the way, I thought that you always locked your front gate." Prakash glared at him and then said, "I must have forgotten!" Raj looked at Hari who said, "Nothing on him except for these." He showed Raj a handkerchief, some keys, a locket on a chain that Hari had removed from around Prakash's neck, a watch and a wallet. Raj nodded and told the constables, "Take him away!"

After the constables had left with Prakash, Raj asked David, "So how do you think we should proceed? He just came out the front door so I think we can look in without triggering any device." He stepped to the front door and peered inside but the place was in darkness. He told Hari to get the flashlights from the car and then he clicked on the torch on his mobile phone and shone it inside the house. He saw the well-furnished sit-out where David and Ramya had interviewed Prakash, but the sitting room door was shut. David told him, "Hang on for a minute while Ramya and I take a look around the house."

David and Ramya walked around the house and they found a shed at the back. They both had the torches on their mobile phones on and now they shone the light inside the shed. They looked at the drum and the other junk and Ramya remarked, "This is just like the shed at the back of Siva's house." David looked over everything carefully without stepping into the shed. "This would make a good hiding place," he told Ramya. Just then Raj and Hari came around the back carrying two powerful torches and they shone the light inside the shed.

Hari started to take a step into the shed but David held him back. "I think we should do the search in daylight," he told Raj. "We can also bring a large tarpaulin big enough to cover the entire front of this shed." Hari said, "That's a good idea. We can hang it from the roof and keep it rolled up, but in case anything happens we can just let it drop and seal it to the walls. We can bring enough tape and sealing solution to do the job." Raj agreed and said, "Yes, that would ensure that if the worst were to happen and we trigger the device, at least the poison won't spread with the wind." Ramya tapped on her phone screen and said, "I'll call the station and get two constables to be posted here right now until the morning." David told Raj, "Let's plan for 8.00 a.m."

David called Rani even though it was very late. When she picked up the phone the first thing she said was, "David! Are you alright?" He frowned and then said, "Of course I am! Why would you..." His voice trailed off and then he said, "Ah! Devika of course!" Rani spoke rapidly and told him in an agitated voice, "Yes, she just phoned me and told me what had happened! The attack this evening! Hari had phoned her and said that he would be late! Then he told her about this attack and that all of you were going into that disaster zone!" David said calmly, "Take a deep breath, Rani, and slow down. Yes, we did go there but we went with full precautions. We all wore the full PPE suits and we are all safe. Sadly I can't say the same for the Shanthi Nagar residents."

Speaking in a more normal voice, Rani asked him, "David, was it very bad?" He sighed and said, "The guy sprayed arsine gas in the area using a fog machine. The people thought that it was the usual corporation man spraying for mosquito control. There are going to be a lot of casualties! If only..." Rani gasped and cried out, "Oh David! I've told you this before but I'll tell you again. You always give of your best but there are times when you cannot save everyone. I want you to always remember that!" He was quiet for a moment and then he told her, "Yes, I remember you spoke to me about this during that psychopath episode when I was depressed over the death of Reshma and the torture of the other two girls and Vicky. It is always hard for me and I always tend to think that if only I had solved the case sooner...but then I think of what you said. I know that you are right and now I mostly don't blame myself, but it's still hard, especially in this case with so many deaths!"

Changing the subject, Rani told him, "But you got the criminal and that is what counts. Devika told me that Hari said if it wasn't for you the man might have got away with it. She said that the central agencies had arrested the wrong man." David took a deep breath and said, "Yes, that's true and Raj has arrested him. Tomorrow morning we are going to search for the evidence and I'm very confident that we will find it." Rani told him, "So think of all the lives that are saved because you have arrested him. Who knows how many lives might have been lost in his next attack!" David said, "Have I told you lately that I love you?" Rani laughed and replied, "You tell me that every night!" David told her soberly, "You have become my rock in life, you know that? When some of these cases get me down then you are always there to pick me up again." They spoke some more and then Rani told him to try and sleep and ended the call.

MAY 19, WEDNESDAY

FINAL ACT

THE NEXT MORNING on the dot at 8.00 a.m. David and Raj arrived at the police station. They took Hari, Ramya, Gopal, and two constables with them and left for Prakash's house. Ramya had procured a large thick tarpaulin sheet and it was loaded in the back of the police van. David, Raj and the two constables went in a police jeep while Hari, Ramya, and Gopal went in the police van. David asked Raj, "Did you inform Inspector Jamal that you had arrested Prakash?" Raj shook his head and replied, "Sometimes even a good and smart man can stick his head in the sand, so I saw no point in telling him anything for now. Let us get the evidence and then I'll inform him."

In the police van, Hari asked Gopal, "So what do you think, will we find the evidence or will Inspector Jamal be proved right that Siva is actually the criminal?" Gopal shrugged and asked him instead, "What do you *think*? Will David be proved right that Prakash is the perpetrator?" Hari was serious as he told him, "We've worked together for many years and I have learned that David's mind works on a different wavelength. I have watched him, in so many seemingly impossible cases, take two or three innocuous items, put them together, and come up with an entire plot! Take this case for example. What made him so sure that Prakash is guilty? Prakash claimed that the caller compared his book and Siva's book, but actually his book was never published! That is something that is so easy to miss for the rest of us in an investigation since it is just part of a conversation, but David is like that. His mind is always quick to spot anything that is odd and then he builds on that."

Ramya remarked, "I think the final odd fact that makes David very sure that we will find the evidence is what he spotted when we arrested Prakash last night. David noted the fact that the gate was not locked." Gopal was curious and asked her, "Why is that relevant?" Ramya told him, "When we called on Prakash the first time to interview him, the gate was locked and we rang the calling bell thrice. We had to wait for more than five minutes before he came to the door." She paused and then added, "My God!

That was just yesterday afternoon! He must have been making his preparations at the time and that was the reason why he took so long to come to the front door." Gopal was still curious and asked her, "But why is the gate being locked or unlocked important?" Ramya said, "When he came to open the gate, he apologised and said that he always kept the gate locked because otherwise unwanted people, selling something or looking for donations, would come to the front door and disturb him. Although we had not commented on the delay or on the gate being locked, Prakash made it a point to explain it. Now that we know that the gate is not usually locked, it highlights his unasked for explanation yesterday."

Hari interrupted and told Gopal, "Now that's the kind of thing I was trying to explain. There's nothing in that incident to make anyone remember it, just the gate being locked, a delay, and an explanation. But it was an unasked for explanation and that would have stuck in David's mind. So last night when we found the gate unlocked, David's mind would have immediately recalled that incident and it would mean that Prakash had lied." Gopal sighed and said, "I get it now. Why would he lie? Because he had only locked the gate since he did not want to be disturbed at *that* time, so he was up to something that he did not want anyone to see. So he just made up an excuse to explain the locked gate in the middle of the day."

They reached the house and Raj asked David, "So how do you think we should proceed, start to take the house apart or start with that shed." David rubbed his chin and said, "Yesterday he took a long time to come to the front door, so..." Ramya interrupted and said, "The locked gate yesterday afternoon, his explanation for it, and the unlocked gate last night. That convinces you that he was working in that shed yesterday!" David raised his eyebrows and stared at her for a long moment. Then he suddenly smiled and told her, "I think I'm going to take you under my wing. Sort of make you my protégé!"

He turned to Raj and said, "That's what I was going to say anyway, so let's go to the shed." But Raj told him, "He could have been working in the house and spent the time hiding everything before coming to the door." David shook his head and replied, "He sat us down in his sit-out and the door to the sitting room was open. If he had to hide something in there then it would have taken much more than five minutes. But you saw the shed last night and you saw the tarpaulin and the other things. All he had to do was to push everything together and cover them with the tarpaulin, five minutes max!"

Raj asked him, "So we won't need to search the house?" David regarded him for a moment and then replied, “I don’t really know. I’m sure the evidence will be in the shed and I’m afraid that he may have rigged a booby trap there. But he may also think that the police would first search the house, so he may have rigged a booby trap there as well. When you do go into the house to search, please be very, very careful.” Turning to Ramya he asked her, “You brought what I asked for?” She told him, “It’s in the van. The constables will get suited up, but before that they will fix the tarpaulin to the roof of the shed.” Raj asked her, “Suited up? You brought the PPE kits?” She nodded and said, “We brought four; two for the constables and the other two are for you and David.” Hari remarked, “Leaders lead from the front! We humble followers will stand well back cowering in fear while you and David take the front row!” Raj shook his head and remarked to David, “He’s been like this from the time he married Devika!”

They went to the back of the house and looked into the shed. The constables meanwhile had gone to a neighbour’s house and borrowed a ladder. They climbed the ladder to the roof of the shed and fixed the tarpaulin there all rolled up with a string hanging down to the ground. Pulling on the string would unroll the tarpaulin and it would drop down to cover the front of the shed. They came down and pulled on the PPE suits and they were ready to go.

David and Raj looked at everything in the shed slowly and carefully. Raj said, "It could be under that tarpaulin at the back. There seems to be a lot of stuff under that." He told the constables, "Start from the entrance. Carefully, and I mean really carefully, pick up each piece of junk and pass it to us. Do not move further until I tell you to do so." He and David then pulled on the PPE suits and the constables began removing the junk one piece at a time.

Suddenly David stopped them and told Hari, "Go to the neighbours and see if they have a long length of water hose. Attach it to a tap there and see if the hose will extend to here. If not, then get another hose and attach it. Now this is important, Hari, when you attach the hose to the tap you must open the tap and close the other end of the hose. When the water builds up in the hose it should still remain attached to the tap, so make sure of that." Hari was listening intently and now he said, "If a gas is released then you want to spray the inside of the shed with water. I get it. I'll get the hose set up, just give me ten minutes." He left and Gopal asked David, "You think that will work?" David shrugged and replied, "Well, it's not foolproof, but water spray will combine with most of the gas and arsenic particles and bring them down to the ground right here. It should help to prevent the spread of the gas."

The two constables had removed most of the old

tyres, tubes, pipes, fans, and some pieces of rope and old sacks by the time Hari came back with the end of a long hose. He had simply tied a piece of rubber tubing to cover the mouth of the hose to keep the water in under pressure. David had made the constables look at each piece of junk from all directions to see if anything was connected to it before he allowed them to lift it up. Finally they got the shed cleared of most of the junk without any untoward incident. All that was left was what was covered with the tarpaulin and the big drum. Raj suggested they take a break as they were sweating profusely in the PPE suits in the summer heat. He and David and the constables took off the suits and found that they were literally soaked in sweat. Ramya sent one of the constables to the police van and he came back with a cooler which held bottles of ice-cold Coca-Cola and Sprite. Raj commended her forethought and she said, “I just thought that with the PPE suits in this heat an ice-cold drink would be very welcome.”

They drank slowly while they looked at what remained in the shed. Raj said, “I think it will be under that tarpaulin. Maybe we can just move that drum to the side and then we can examine that place more easily.” Hari immediately moved to the drum, but as he laid his hands on it David shouted, “Stop! Hari, stop!” Hari froze and slowly turned his head to look at David. "Come away slowly from there, Hari," David told him in a more normal voice. Carefully, as though he was walking on eggshells, Hari came out of the shed. Raj looked at David and asked him, "You think it may be in the drum? But then it will be contained, wouldn't it?" David just kept staring at the drum while he thought and he did not answer Raj. Then his face cleared and he told Raj, "That drum will have some weight. I am thinking that it would be a simple matter for an engineer to rig a trap that would be set off when that drum is shifted." Raj frowned while he thought and then he said, "I guess that makes sense, but we can narrow down the possibilities now I think."

He told the two constables to suit up again but then said, "First we will pull down the tarpaulin to cover the front of the shed. You two get up there and make sure that it is sealed on top. We've got tape and a sticking solution so you can use that."

One of the constables said, "We have already done that, Sir."

Raj nodded and went on, "Then we seal the right side against the wall and then seal the bottom to the ground, leaving only the left side unsealed. Hari will also suit up and he will stand by the left side holding the water hose. You two will go in there fully suited up and you will take off that tarpaulin and see what is under it. In case the gas is set off,

Hari will remove the cap on the water hose and throw it to you. He will then quickly but lightly seal the last opening, which is the left side, but only with tape. You will take the hose and start spraying water over the area from where you can see the gas emanating and also spray the air around you. Keep spraying until there is no more gas in the air and then push open the left side of this tarpaulin and come out. If nothing happens after you remove the tarpaulin, then as before, you carefully check and remove each piece of junk one by one and place it here near the entrance."

So that's what they did. Hari was watching through a gap at the left side and he kept up a running commentary for the others who had fallen back about ten feet from the shed.

The constables removed the tarpaulin and nothing happened. They very carefully and cautiously removed each piece of junk one by one and still nothing happened. It took them more than half an hour and then finally they came to the entrance and Hari let them out. Raj told them to remove their suits and take a break with some cold drinks. Then he and Hari removed the sealing from the bottom of the tarpaulin and pulled it to one side and taped it to the wall. All of them began shifting the junk and the tarpaulin that covered it out of the shed until the shed held only the drum. Raj, Hari, and David got down on their haunches and carefully examined the bottom of the drum resting on the floor.

It was Hari who said, "I think that there's a slab under the drum. Look here and here, you can see the outline of the edges of the slab. It's been placed so that it sits flush with the rest of the floor."

Raj and David looked and Hari said, "I bet that there's a pit under the drum covered with a slab. The drum is placed on top of the slab."

Raj and David both agreed and Raj said, "So if the drum is shifted then something happens and the trap is triggered?"

David was rubbing his chin and now he said, "It has to be something simple if the trap is to be sprung by shifting the drum. Now, for the gas to be produced, the arsenic must fall into some acid. At least that's what I've been reading on the net."

Hari remarked, "So maybe a hole in the drum and a hole in the slab. The arsenic will fall from the drum through the hole in the slab into the acid which should be in the pit."

Raj was sceptical and said, "If there is a hole in the drum then the arsenic will have already fallen through the hole and shifting the drum wouldn't make any difference."

Suddenly David's eyes lit up and he said, "Wait, Raj's right. There can't be a hole in the drum. I'm just thinking that you can't have a simple device that will trigger the arsenic to fall into the acid under the drum when the drum is shifted."

Raj said, "So then what?"

David told him softly, "What if the arsenic has already been dropped in the acid and the gas is already there waiting to be released?"

Hari took a deep breath and exclaimed, "The drum is holding the gas in the pit!"

David nodded and said, "Look closely and you will see that the bottom of the drum sits flush against the floor, there is no gap there. The bottom of the drum is flat and even and the floor is also flat and even."

Raj exclaimed, "That's it, that's it! It has to be! So we can keep the hose ready and as we shift the drum we can unleash the water. Will that work?"

David sighed and said, "It should, but then the water will be contaminated and that will have to be contained. We are out of our element with something like this. I think you have to call in the disaster management team and let them know what we suspect. They are the experts and they will take it from here."

Raj pulled out his phone and said, "They are already here and they are working in Shanthi Nagar. I know the man in charge and I'll give him a call now."

Within half an hour a van pulled up to the

house and four members of the disaster management team got down. Raj took them to the back of the house and showed them the shed and the drum. He explained what they expected to find under the drum and he also explained the measures they had taken so far to clear all the other junk out of the shed. The leader of the team, Arul Ram, scratched his head and said, "I must say that for amateurs the idea is ingenious, but if you take down the gas with a water spray then you also have to deal with the contaminated water and this entire shed as well."

Raj told him, "David figured as much and that's why we called you."

Raj introduced him to David and the others and Arul Ram said, "Well, with David Joseph here no wonder you guys figured all this out." He raised his hands and said with a smile, "I don't mean to put you guys down, it's just that with his brains..." He turned to David and asked him, "You're sure that's what we will find when we shift that drum?"

David shrugged and told him, "I think he would booby trap the evidence. We are also sure, after seeing that there is a slab under that drum, that the evidence is hidden there in a pit. Whether he will use arsine gas or something else for the booby trap I cannot say. You will have to be prepared for anything I guess."

Arul Ram considered that and then said, "You

are basing your thinking on the fact that he has arsenic which he used in the water tank and also the fact that he used arsine gas, or what we are assuming is arsine gas, in Shanthi Nagar. We are also quite sure that he used a fog machine to disperse the gas." He paused while he thought and then said, "I like that thinking and I agree. From what we are finding in Shanthi Nagar, I think he used gas and a liquefied form sprayed under pressure. That's why there were deaths within a short period of time for those who were directly exposed because they would have inhaled and most probably swallowed some of the liquefied form. Tiny droplets on your lips, you tend to just lick your lips!" He paused again and then said, "This guy must have modified the fog machine otherwise he could not have done this using a standard fog machine."

Ramya told him, "He was an engineer before he became a writer."

Arul Ram threw up his hands and said, "Well, that explains it! Now you guys please go home or to the police station or wherever and leave us to get this done. By the way, I'll keep the tarpaulin and the hose since I'm also going to be using your idea to start with." He told Raj, "I will phone you and send you pictures of what we find, but we will have to decontaminate everything before you can lay your hands on it."

Raj thanked him and said, “Photographs will be enough for now, thank you.” They left the house and returned to the police station.

When they entered the police station, they found Inspector Jamal waiting for them. “What’s this I hear that you’ve arrested the other writer, Prakash?” he asked Raj. David and the others walked to Gopal’s office and Raj told Inspector Jamal, “Come with us and I’ll explain. Right now I need to just sit down and have a cup of strong coffee.”

Inspector Gopal stopped and told a constable, “Strong coffee for all of us, please.” He remarked to David, “After this morning I think we all need it!”

They seated themselves in the office and Inspector Jamal again asked Raj, “So you’ve arrested the writer Prakash?”

Raj said, “Yes, we are sure that he is the one who carried out these two attacks.”

Inspector Jamal asked him, “Has he confessed?”

Raj shook his head and said, “I have not interrogated him as yet. We’ve been searching for evidence at his house and I will interrogate him once we have the evidence.”

Inspector Jamal frowned and said, “So you don’t have any evidence, the suspect has not confessed, but still you have arrested him?”

Raj asked him in a stern official voice, “Just what

are you trying to say, Inspector? Are you questioning my right to arrest a suspect?"

Inspector Jamal immediately became contrite and said, "I'm sorry SP, I did not mean it that way! I arrested a suspect who had confessed and you said that I had the wrong man, but here you are arresting a suspect who has not confessed and against whom you have no evidence. I guess I'm a bit confused and that's the reason why I am asking."

Raj told him, "First of all, I did not say that you had the wrong man. That was David, and I only suggested that you listen to his point of view. You dismissed my suggestion and instead told me that I could listen to him and do whatever I wanted since I was in a different department from yours."

Inspector Jamal shifted his feet and looked embarrassed. He turned to David and told him, "I suppose I was a bit rude last night and I apologise for that."

David smiled at him and said, "Sit down, Inspector, no need to apologise. That was your big moment when you made the announcement that you had arrested the man responsible and that the man had confessed. An open and shut case for you and I shot down the idea and told you that you had arrested the wrong man. You just responded as any normal human being would in that situation, so don't let it worry you."

Inspector Jamal sighed and sat down. "If you don't mind, can I hear your point of view now?"

David said, "Of course, Inspector, but first tell me what has changed since last night to make you doubt Siva's confession."

Inspector Jamal looked at him in surprise and exclaimed, "But I never said that I..." His voice trailed off and with a look of resignation he said, "But you are *the* David Joseph so why would I be surprised?"

David glanced at Ramya but she had a bland look on her face, although he detected a mischievous glint in her eyes. He asked Inspector Jamal, "Has Siva started raving about his mother?"

Jamal again had a look of surprise on his face as he said, "How the hell...I'm sorry! Yes, he is raving about how he would now be the one in control. Sometimes he talks as though his mother is standing in front of him! I think he's gone totally insane!"

David shook his head and said, "That was faster than I thought. The man needs immediate therapy and treatment. If you would release him, I will talk to his mother and get him the treatment that he desperately needs."

Inspector Jamal agreed and again asked him, "So will you tell me now why you believe that Prakash is guilty?"

So David told him everything. As he was explaining things to Inspector Jamal, Raj jumped up and said, "David, look at this! Arul Ram has sent me these pictures."

They all crowded around him and saw the pictures of the pit with the evidence in it. Then there were individual pictures of the fog machine and the cans that were used to store the arsenic and the acid. There were pictures of the khaki clothing, the black plastic that was used to change the appearance of the scooter, and the fake licence plates. There was a message from Arul Ram with the pictures which said, "David was right. The gas was in the pit! There was a hole in the slab and we managed to cap it before the gas could pour out. Then we attached a suction device to the hole and siphoned off the gas before opening the pit."

David stood up and told Raj, "Okay, you have all you need to convict him now. But if you wouldn't mind a word of advice..."

Raj gave him a look and David said, "Sorry! Just show him the pictures of the evidence and commiserate with him about how his plea for enhancement of security over the water supply was ignored by the authorities. You will get an immediate and full confession from him."

So that was what Raj did and he got his confession.

AFTERMATH

INSPECTOR GOPAL, Sub-Inspector Ramya, Inspector Hari, and Superintendent of Police Raj Kumar received commendations and medals from the police department and the state government. The Chief Minister wanted to honour David Joseph at a public function, but David refused. When Ramya asked him why he had not accepted the gratitude of the state government, all he would say was, "Maybe if I had been able to prevent the second attack..."

The people of Ram Nagar, Vivek Nagar, and Anbu Nagar never forgot that horrible Friday. In each residential colony, they put up a shrine to honour the dead and above the names of the dead was a plaque that read, *'Victims of an insane attack.'* May

14th was remembered by the residents as the day when insanity struck their colonies.

Little Suganya never again disobeyed her parents. The two young sons of Sarala and Rakesh were brought up by their relatives. Ramya kept track of their lives and after six months she realised that the trauma of that day, seeing their parents dying, had not left them. She told David and he arranged for them to attend therapy sessions. Ameena died a year after the attack due to health issues related to arsenic poisoning. Her two sons survived but they had serious health issues for a long time. Kamala of Anbu Nagar was honoured by the local district administration for her quick thinking that had saved the lives of her neighbours. Little Divya's body was cremated, but her mother Sanjana put up a small shrine in their home to honour and remember her little daughter. The image of the three-year-old girl lying dead in her bed in a pool of faeces and vomit haunted Ramya for a long time until she finally went to David for extended therapy sessions.

It took nearly a month to decontaminate Shanthi Nagar and for a distance of almost two kilometres downwind from there. Geetha gave birth to a baby girl, and although they were Hindus, she and her husband named the child Fatima to honour the lady whose neurosis saved her life. Vijay died that night while his wife Shanthi and their nine-year-old daughter survived, although with serious health issues. Shanthi received good compensation from the government, while the trust run by David's stepdaughter Revathi took care of her daughter's education. Gauri survived while her sister Girija died and for a long time Gauri was tormented by the thought that she could have saved her sister if only she had insisted that her sister come home with her that night. When the residents of Shanthi Nagar were finally able to come back to their homes, they put up a shrine to commemorate the dead. The residents always spoke of that night as the night of silent terror. At the shrine, above the names of those who had died, there was a plaque that read, *'May 18, the night that silent terror struck this colony.'*

The government made a lot of announcements and undertook serious security measures to safeguard the potable water supply from the reservoirs right up to the overhead water tanks. Drones could not be used in public spaces without official permission. In response to the demands of the public, a rule was passed that made it mandatory for any corporation or government employee, who entered a colony for mosquito fogging or for any other purpose, to produce their government identity proof whenever anyone asked for it.

EPILOGUE

TYING UP ENDS

INSPECTOR JAMAL RELEASED Siva but not before David had given him some tablets to calm him down since he was raving when they saw him. David and Ramya took him to his house and they left him upstairs lying down in his bed. He was very calm and docile by that time and he said, "I think I'll just sleep for a while if you don't mind." They came down and spoke to his mother and father. When David told Siva's mother what was wrong with her son she vehemently denied everything and was angry. "That's rubbish!" she told David. "I'm a good mother and I have looked after my son well. To even suggest that I drove him insane is...is..." She stuttered and her husband said, "Is the truth!"

She glared at him but he told her, "Don't waste

those looks on me, it won't work. I guess I'm to blame for this state of affairs. I've always believed in peace at any cost and so I put up with all your nonsense for all these years. You thought you controlled me but you never have and you never will. I just don't like fighting and so I never bother to argue with you, but I never realised the harm that my attitude did to my son." She started to shout and he told her calmly, "If you don't shut up then I will divorce you and you can live on your own. From now on I will take care of my son and you will just take care of this house. The choice is yours!" He turned to David and said, "Tell me what to do and I will do it, but I beg of you to please save my son."

David and Ramya were at Raj's house and Ramya was saying, "I've been thinking about what you said. I'm 24 years old now and I'm wondering if I will be able to go back to college where I would be surrounded by youngsters as my classmates. Law enforcement is in my blood, so I'm wondering if I can make the switch."

David told her, "You won't be making a switch. You will study psychology and you will specialise in criminal psychology and then you will join the crime branch. You are a very good detective and I believe you should remain on the force. But once you major in criminal psychology, then your natural skills will be enhanced and you will be a better detective for it."

She agreed and David made the arrangements with his stepdaughter Revathi for a full scholarship for Ramya.

Before going back home, he visited Hariharan and told him, "You're a nice guy and I've looked you up. You've done yeoman service for your community, but there's one thing that could one day spoil it all for you and that's your anger issues."

Hariharan gave him a rueful grin and said, "I know, and I've been trying my best to get control of it but I don't think I'm succeeding."

David gave him a card and said, "This man has many years of experience in anger management and he is the best one to help you." He paused and added, "At least in my opinion."

Hariharan laughed and told him, "Your opinion is good enough for me! Thank you, David, I will definitely go and see him."

Then he suddenly added, "But I wish more of my community had anger as well!"

David gave him a steady look and said, "Anger by itself has never solved anything in this life. But anger that is controlled and channelled can achieve much. The trick in that is the control and the channelling."

Hariharan was thoughtful for a while and then

said, "Something like what happened to achieve the police reforms in this country? It started with that vigilante group from what I heard. It was rumoured at the time that the group was made up of rape victims and others who were affected by this horrendous crime against women. I suppose that anger against rape fuelled those vigilantes at first. But the way they went about it surprised me at the end."

David asked him, "Why did it surprise you?"

Hariharan told him, "At first, like most others who followed those events, I thought it was just some random attacks. You know, some victims who just thought that enough was enough. If the law could not give them justice then they would get justice themselves. But as it went on it became obvious that it was a well-planned strategy. It fired up the imagination of the people and soon everyone joined in and it became a mass movement. At the end of it all I realised that maybe the actual goal of that campaign was to force the authorities to enact police reforms, and it worked."

David said, "So what are you actually saying?"

Hariharan frowned and then said slowly, "The authorities only paid lip service to the problem of crime against women in this country until the vigilante action changed all that. The crimes against Dalits are as bad as the crimes against women. So I'm just thinking that maybe only a campaign like that can finally get justice for the Dalits; fuel and channel the anger!"

David said softly, "But for that to happen it would take a great deal of planning and most of all a committed leader."

Hariharan stared at him with an unfocused gaze and murmured, "Yes, a committed leader." Suddenly he shook his head and his eyes came into focus again. He told David, "But thanks so much for taking this interest in me. I will definitely make an appointment for my anger management."

As David was leaving, Hariharan asked him, "I heard that you found the man responsible for those deadly attacks. So can you tell me if he was just totally mad or if he was a terrorist?"

David shrugged and said, "Neither, it was just the work of an insane mind!"

ABOUT THE AUTHOR

Terence Newnes was born in south India. He dropped out of college and during the 70s and 80s he worked in fabrication, machine shops, and tool rooms. He then worked a short stint in Ethiopia. At the age of 43 he became a certified medical transcriptionist and worked in Toledo, Ohio as a medical transcriptionist, editor, and finally shift team lead. He started his own business of call center and data entry in 2006. During the pandemic and lockdown he lost his business and went broke, but he never lost hope. He started writing, which was a childhood dream, and he has never stopped.

To learn more about Terence Newnes and discover

more Next Chapter authors, visit our website at www.nextchapter.pub.

An Insane Mind
ISBN: 978-4-82419-759-7
Large Print

Published by
Next Chapter
2-5-6 SANNO
SANNO BRIDGE
143-0023 Ota-Ku, Tokyo
+818035793528

3rd September 2024

Milton Keynes UK
Ingram Content Group UK Ltd.
UKHW031157251124
451529UK00003B/195

9 784824 197597